MW01179080

STOOPID

Ed & Bo
Take on the World

MISADVENTURE #6

Laura McGehee

EPIC
Press

Ed & Bo Take on the World
Stoopid: Book #6

Written by Laura McGehee

Copyright © 2016 by Abdo Consulting Group, Inc.

Published by EPIC Press™
PO Box 398166
Minneapolis, MN 55439

Cover design by Dorothy Toth
Images for cover art obtained from iStockPhoto.com
Edited by Ryan Hume

LIBRARY OF CONGRESS CATALOGING-IN-PUBLICATION DATA

McGehee, Laura.
Ed & Bo take on the world / Laura McGehee.
p. cm. — (Stoopid ; #6)
Summary: Ed & Bo are back where they started, without a business and in their par-
ent's garage. Ultimately, the young men must decide what to do with their company
and their lives.
ISBN 978-1-68076-062-0 (hardcover)
1. High schools—Fiction. 2. High school seniors—Fiction. 3. Interpersonal
relations—Fiction. 4. Friendship—Fiction. 5. Graduation (School—Fiction.
6. Young adult fiction. I. Title.
[Fic]—dc23
2015903985

To all the Ed's and Bo's I grew up with,
May you never entirely forget the idiocy of youth.

"**N**o, dude, you are not hearing me," Bo shouted at the top of his lungs over the sounds of after school traffic and an alarmingly loud bulldozer.

"What?" Ed shouted back. For the first time, his lack of hearing was due to the environment and not to his childhood affliction of swimmer's ear.

"I said, you are NOT hearing me," Bo repeated.

"What?"

"You. Are. Not—"

"WHAT?"

The bulldozer stopped its all-encompassing destruction for a blessed few moments of respite, and they were able to once again hear the sounds of high school students scurrying home with the increased frenzy of only a few weeks of classes left before summer.

"I *said* that you are not hearing me," Bo said.

"Well, yeah, I wasn't."

"No, but I mean in the metaphorical sense," Bo said. His long and wild hair was tamed into a sensible man bun, resting at the very nape of his neck. Now that the promise of summer air and sun was upon them, Bo's complexion was an astounding five shades darker than normal, and his tank tops and shorts inadvertently showed off his accidentally well-shaped limbs. He had shaved his poorly formed beard from his wolf days, which revealed the surprisingly strong jawline underneath. He sat back in the floral, thrift-store deck chair and turned his face toward the sun, taking a deep hit from their joint.

"I never should have taught you that word," Ed said with a laugh and reaching out to take the joint. He propped up his legs on the railing, readjusting his hoodie to make sure it covered his arms, face, and all of his sensitively pale skin. In the warmer months, Ed's skin reddened rather than tanned. When Ed exhaled a long stream of smoke and subsequently fogged up his glasses, he wiped them in his shirt.

"I learned it all on my own, thank you very much!" Bo retorted. "Well, the wolves taught it to me, really."

"The wolves taught you more than twelve years of public education did," Ed drawled.

"Stop distracting me from my point of you *not* hearing me!" Bo said, accepting the joint back from Ed. "You see, the whole thing about llamas and alpacas is that—"

With a dull roar, the bulldozer started once more, and both boys gave up. They were lounging on the roof of their former high school, Interius Montgomery High, and they were not enjoying their new hangout spot in the slightest. It was the dawn of June and the beginning of the end of the school year. A year prior, the boys had been in the final throes of the Young Rising Entrepreneur Competition and on the verge of the rest of their exciting lives. Now, they were smoking on the rooftop of their former institution of learning and hoping they did not run into any old teachers. Both boys had realized that sometimes a year did not change that much.

When the bulldozers stopped once more, Bo reared up to continue his point about llamas and alpacas, but the door opened with a resounding clang. Both boys paled, which was more of a feat for Bo's olive skin than Ed's, and then quickly jumped to hide the evidence of their weed. Even if it was legal in their state, they knew it was not encouraged to smoke on the roof of their former high school. The sharp eyes and soft face of Natalie looked back at the two of them. She shook her head and laughed.

"You scared the shit out of us!" Ed shouted.

"You guys really, *really* need to get another place to hang," Natalie said with a scoff. She marched towards the two of them, sitting down in the third lawn chair and unloading her backpack with a groan. Since the half-shaved head incident of a few weeks prior, Natalie had shaved her head in its entirety without warning one morning. She now had slight magenta stubble across her head that Ed continued to try to mock, even though he knew deep down that it looked pretty cool. Bo, however, found it entirely mesmerizing. But then again, she had captivated him for longer than he could even remember. Luckily for Bo, they would keep seeing Natalie for at least the next two weeks. Until her graduation, she was just as chained to the institution of public learning as the rest of her classmates; however, she compensated by coming up to the roof at the end of the day to smoke.

"But this one is so convenient for you to join us," Bo said, and Natalie smirked back at him. They held eye contact for a few moments, and then abruptly dropped it. Bo shifted in his seat and struggled with how he was existing, feeling Ed's eyes burning into him. He crossed his hands, and then uncrossed them. He crossed his legs, and then uncrossed them. Bo and Natalie had yet to resolve the unresolved ending of affairs between them a few months prior. Things had happened so fast—from storming the Square One office in New York, to trying to reclaim their business, to eating a lot of pizza, to returning home in shame, they really hadn't had any time to talk about what they were or whatever else they were supposed to talk about at a time like this. Bo wasn't really the best at articulating these sorts of things, and Natalie seemed to be defiantly waiting for him to say something on the topic before she shared her thoughts. In the meantime, Bo remembered his feelings toward her every time he saw her, and then remembered that Ed knew about his feelings toward Natalie, and then strongly felt the urge to hide.

"You guys are idiots," Ed said under his breath,

but the starting and stopping of the bulldozer's engine masked it.

"What the *hell* is all this noise?" Bo asked in the voice of a terrible stand-up comedian, in a clever ploy to change the subject.

"They're building a new senior courtyard," Natalie said with a shrug. "There was that huge spider infestation. Like *huge.*"

Ed shuddered with the memories of the creepy creatures that had dominated the senior hang out place, and Bo paled instantly.

"They're displacing all of those spiders?!" Bo shouted. "No way. They can't do that."

"They're just spiders, dude," Ed said.

"Yeah, but they were *our* spiders!" Bo insisted. "Who is in charge of horrifically removing all these poor defenseless creatures from their home?"

"Guess," Natalie said flatly.

"The Walcot Foundation?" Bo responded, just as flatly. Natalie's eyes said it all.

"Of course," Bo responded bitterly. "Well I'm going to save them."

"You need to save yourselves first," Natalie quipped. She grabbed the joint from Ed, who rolled his eyes but let her take it anyway.

"Anyways, Natalie," Ed said sharply to his sister. "We can't get another hangout place because we were entirely swindled out of our rightful one."

Natalie sighed heavily and glared down at the joint in her hands. "I'm still pissed about that."

Cameron had acquisitioned their garage under the control of CotLaw Inc., due to some shady contracts Ed and Bo had accidentally signed once upon a time. They had returned from the failed New York showdown to find it under lock and key, and not just one lock and one key, but many locks and many keys. There was also a very stern security guard simply named "Four," who stood with his arms crossed outside the garage at all hours of every day. Ed and Bo had tried to watch him to see when he went to the bathroom and stuff like that, but inevitably fell asleep before they saw him move. Bo suspected he might be a robot. Natalie had tried calling the cops—but the boys had unfortunately lawfully bequeathed the premises to CotLaw, as the bored officer patronizingly explained to them.

"Mom is going to freak out," Ed said. "I'm definitely going to blame you."

"Are you kidding? I'm not the one who created this whole business and signed that shitty contract and befriended Cameron and all that in the first place!" Natalie said. Bo nodded along with her.

"She's kinda got a point, dude."

Ed shrugged. "Whatever. I just don't really understand how he did it."

"Me neither," Bo said. "I mean yeah, we signed a few contracts, but how did he singlehandedly ruin our lives?"

"Your lives aren't ruined," Natalie said with visibly fake warmth. "Look at you two," she said. The boys did indeed look at themselves up and down and then at each other. Bo chuckled when he saw

Ed's insistence on multiple layers even though it was on the verge of heavy-sweat weather, and also realized for the first time that Ed's chin had a new sort of angle to it and his chest seemed to expand more than before—maybe he was becoming a real adult. Then he noticed that Ed was wearing the baby blue hoodie that rang some sort of bell deep in his mind.

"Dude! Is that Cameron's hoodie?"

Ed smiled sheepishly. "All my other clothes are dirty, or suits."

Bo thought about it, and then shrugged, because the On the House Hoodies that Cameron had given them were quite nice, even if they were evil. Ed looked back at Bo, laughing at his mismatch of colors—a bright green tank and bright orange pants, with no visible shoes to round out the outfit. He thought that Bo's face and eyes looked a bit wiser, but his clothes made him look like a complete dweeb. They both looked at each other and chuckled, and Natalie laughed as well.

"That was a joke, you guys. Your lives pretty much are ruined—sitting on the roof of your old high school, smoking joints, and watching construction? What would Belfroy say?"

"Do not bring him up," Bo said sharply. "He is always listening."

Natalie rolled her eyes once more. "You guys are depressed."

"Are not!" Ed said.

"You totally are. I got a four on the AP psych exam, I think I know what depression looks like."

"You wanna talk psych? Dear god, what is going on with your head?" Ed spat out. Natalie rubbed her hand across her stubble and her eyes sparked with the kind of flame that only Ed's criticisms could elicit.

"It's edgy, dude, I don't want to have to explain it again," Natalie said with a sigh.

"Mom is going to kill you," Ed repeated. "First the garage, and now this?"

"Oh, that reminds me, Mom called me last

night to tell me that I am in charge of everything, and just because you ran a business and went to college and dropped out of both, that doesn't mean you're older or wiser than me."

"Mom did not say that."

"She said something sort of like that," Natalie argued. "She also agreed with me that you're a loser and I'm the favorite child."

Ed and Natalie continued to bicker for quite some time. Since Ms. DeLancey had left on a business trip a few weeks ago, the two could barely be in the same room without yelling at each other. Nobody had time to question what globe-collecting job had taken Ms. DeLancey away on business, because bickering was very time-consuming. Finally, Bo interrupted with something he had been trying to say for quite some time.

"I like your hair, Natalie."

"Thank you."

"Of course you do," Ed scoffed. Bo playfully shoved Ed, and Ed shoved him back, and even though Bo kept trying, he never got around to making his point about the difference between a llama and an alpaca.

Ed stared at the vast array of greasy-menu options before him on Al's menu, and Bo found himself staring at yet another flower painting on the wall— or maybe it was the same one, but it was hard to be certain. Natalie sat across from them in the booth, doing her best to catch their waitress' attention.

"I missed Al's," Bo said dreamily, staring at the flower petals and getting lost in the spirals.

"I am so hungry," Natalie complained. "Where the hell is our waitress?"

"It looks . . . busier than usual?" Ed asked. Al's Diner, the lone outlet in their town for greasy and all-traditional American diner food, did indeed look busier than when they had last eaten here. Al's was the go-to place for the type of food you didn't want your Mom to know you were eating, and luckily, Ms. DeLancey was away on business. Tonight the diner was packed and thriving.

"Yeah, they brought in gluten-free options a few weeks ago and it has really changed stuff," Natalie said. Bo jerked a bit at the mention of gluten, because he strongly believed that gluten did not exist.

"Oh yeah? Dying for your tofu-gluten-free-dog-thing?" Ed said mockingly.

"For your information, it's called a Tofurkey sandwich on rye-less rye bread and it's amazing," Natalie retorted back. "And I want to order it! Are you guys ready?"

"Always," Bo drawled.

"Just go and get her attention. It can't be that hard," Ed said in the tone he reserved exclusively for his little sister. Natalie turned to look at him blankly.

"What the hell do you think I've been doing?" she asked. She turned back around and continued searching for their waitress.

"You know, it's really not that hard," Ed continued for Bo, who was only half listening and mostly lost in the flowers once more. "You just wave your hand and say, 'Hey! Ready for food!' If you'd lived in the Big City, as we call it, you'd know a bit more about how to get attention—"

"Oh my god, shut up," Natalie said. "I don't want to hear anything more about your stupid business and fake adulthood." Then she slowly turned to Ed, smiling a devilish sort of smile. "Got her attention."

"Great," Ed said. "Finally."

"Hi there, guys, sorry for the wait. Oh. Oh! Hello!" the waitress said. Ed and Bo both turned to see none other than Hayley Plotinsky looking back at them, also known as the love of Ed's life once upon a time, the same one who had shot him down terribly at Summer Slam.

"Hi!" Ed shouted a bit too loudly.

"Hello!" Bo yelled just as loudly, to mask Ed's weirdness.

"Hayley!" Natalie said warmly, standing up to hug her. Hayley awkwardly hugged her back, and then smiled at both of the boys.

"Well, have you had a good . . . uh, time since Summer Sla—uh, graduation?" she asked uncomfortably.

"Yes. Great time," Ed said mechanically. A long pause of silence, and then Hayley continued.

"I heard you were in New York?"

"Yes," Ed said. "Well, kind of."

"In a sense, for a little," Bo amended. Natalie grinned from ear to ear as she watched this discomfort unfold. Hayley shifted back and forth on her feet, still smiling at the boys but looking very much like she did not want to be there.

"How have you been?" Ed asked.

"Oh, really good! I'm home for the summer from Dartmouth and saving up money for a semester abroad next year," she said. Natalie nodded and shot a pointed glance at the two boys.

"Wow! You've really got your shit together, huh?"

"Uh, I guess so?" Hayley said. "But nothing like you business moguls. Still making a ton of money with Square One?"

Ed, Bo, and this time even Natalie all reddened. Ed mumbled something incoherently, and Hayley looked down at her notepad.

"Okay. Yeah. So, what can I get you guys today?"

When she left, Ed groaned and sunk down in the booth. "Even when we're not in high school anymore, I can't talk to her like a normal person."

"Took the words right out of my mouth," Natalie said with a smirk. "Also, I can't believe she's on summer vacation already. That's so unfair."

"Thus are the perks of not being a child, Natalie," Ed said. Before Natalie could retort, Bo jerked upright.

"Speaking of not being in high school anymore, is that . . . " Bo said. "It is! Hey! Hoodie Joseph!" He stood up from the booth and started to yell across the diner. Everyone turned to look, and when Hoodie Joseph turned around, he immediately paled and walked toward the kitchen. "No! You're going the wrong way! I'm over here!" Bo called. Ed tried to shush Bo, but to no avail. "Hoodie Joseph! It's us! Bo! And Ed! And Natalie!" Finally, Hoodie Joseph looked over toward them and gave a half-hearted wave. He walked with heavy feet towards their booth.

"Sup, guys," he said without enthusiasm.

"Hoodie Joseph!" Bo said once more.

"Hoodie Joseph," Ed repeated. "Where's your hoodie?"

"That's really the only thing you guys know about me, huh?" Hoodie Joseph said without inflection. Ed and Bo both made sounds of protest.

"It's Joseph now, anyways," he said flatly. Natalie meekly raised her hand to wave at Joseph.

"Hey, Joseph."

"Natalie," he said with a curt nod. "Look, I really have to get back to—"

"Wait," Ed said, the wheels in his head turning. "Can you tell us a little bit about getting fired? Natalie mentioned it but—"

"I really can't," Joseph said as he looked around the diner. "Anyways, I've gotta go."

Joseph stared to walk away, and Bo yelled once more, "Wait!"

Joseph stopped and slowly turned around.

"I'm sorry, dude," Bo said softly. "I know you put college on hold to move to New York with us, and I'm sorry it didn't work out."

"Me too," Ed added.

"Thanks," Joseph said. "Nice hoodie," he said to Ed. Joseph walked away and back into the kitchen, leaving the group staring after him. They received their food shortly afterwards, so they didn't really have time to discuss why Joseph was acting the way he was. Ed and Bo could certainly sense that there was something amiss. But then again, a chocolate milkshake, waffle fries, and a Tofurkey sandwich on rye-less rye are good distractions. When they had eaten their food, drank their shakes, and started to feel the grease settle into their stomachs in the most comforting way possible, Natalie cleared her throat.

"Guys, I brought you two here for a reason."

"I drove us here," Ed pointed out.

"Well, yeah, but like in the *metaphorical sense* I brought you two here for a reason. And that reason is to talk about your future."

"You sound *exactly* like Belfroy," Ed said with a groan. "Next thing we know, you're gonna be telling us to 'hang in there.'"

"And you'll be dripping oil and malfunctioning and shit," Bo added. When Ed looked over at him, Bo sighed. "I will prove that he is a robot if it is the last thing that I do!"

Natalie stood up abruptly. "Okay. That's it. I've had enough of this," she said as she gestured to the two boys. "I know this whole not caring about anything is your thing, but you two just got your very lucrative business stolen from you and you don't even seem to mind."

"Of course, we do!" Bo said.

"That's all I can think about," Ed said.

"Well then, act like it!" she yelled. When the patrons around them turned to look, Natalie cleared her throat purposefully. "But anyways, I know you won't really listen to me so I brought someone else to talk to you."

Ed and Bo turned to look at each other, eyes darting around the room in search of the mystery agent.

"Is it Mom?" Ed asked anxiously.

"Or Hoodie Joseph—sorry, Joseph—again?"

Natalie shook her head. "I'm sorry guys, but I really had to do this. This is for your own good." She made brief eye contact with Bo and then turned away, walking out the door and into the warm air that waited beyond. Ed and Bo sat in the booth, fidgeting.

"Should we leave?" Ed asked.

"This must be what a blind date feels like," Bo said. They continued to dart their eyes anxiously around the diner, so they didn't even notice when a cloaked figure walked through the door toward their table. They did notice, however, when the robotic voice they would recognize anywhere sounded from behind them.

"Hello, boys."

Ed and Bo turned around, gulping as they did so and feeling a cold freeze run through their systems. None other Belfroy was staring back at them. He sat down gingerly, removing his coat to reveal a yellow sweatshirt beneath. He grinned the same manic grin that had fueled the theory that Belfroy is a robot in the first place.

"Hi," Ed said blankly.

"Hello," Bo said.

"This meeting is about your future. And that neither of you have one, right now, that is."

Ed and Bo looked at each other and gulped.

2

"**Look, we know the whole thing about** college and how we should go there and—" Ed began, but Belfroy just simply held up his hand.

"Oh no, this isn't going to be about college. College isn't for everyone," Belfroy said abruptly. "That's a conversation for another day." He looked back and forth from Ed to Bo, both of whom couldn't help but feel like they were back in Belfroy's guidance office once more. Bo squirmed in his seat and shifted and re-shifted his legs; Ed polished his glasses repeatedly and sweated more than he would like to admit. They sat in their booth and looked back at Belfroy's dark eyes and unchanging smile. They hoped that they wouldn't get detention.

"Do you boys remember the Young Rising Entrepreneur Competition?" Belfroy asked. The boys looked at each other with wary eyes.

"Why, did we forget to turn in a paper or something?" Bo asked suspiciously.

"No, we definitely turned everything in. You can't stop us from graduating now," Ed said.

"That's not what this is about!" Belfroy said, his voice raising a few octaves. When Ed and Bo stared back at him, he cleared his throat with a cough. "Sorry. But if you would just let me finish, that's not what this meeting is for."

"Then why are we here?" Bo asked. Belfroy looked at the two of them, and then around the diner. He slowly leaned in, and Ed and Bo leaned in, too.

"I have reason to suspect that the Young Rising Entrepreneur Competition was rigged," Belfroy said in his tried and true monotone. Ed couldn't help but laugh. Bo thought he was missing something, so he laughed as well. Belfroy continued to stare at them, unwavering.

"That is not a joke," he said. "I have never made a joke."

Ed and Bo slowly stopped laughing.

"How do you know?" Ed asked.

"Why does it matter?" Bo wondered. Belfroy smiled and continued.

"Excellent questions, both of them," Belfroy said. "Well, I was going back over some records the other day."

"You were just going over our records? Out of the blue?" Ed interrupted.

"What, like our academic records? The shit our teachers wrote about us?" Bo asked.

"No, it was just some old files and I was looking at them and—"

"I don't understand why you were looking at our records specifically, though," Ed repeated. He turned to Bo. "We finished all our requirements, I swear."

"Yeah," Bo agreed. "And you already gave us our diplomas so you can't take them back."

Belfroy sighed and looked the two of them in the eyes. "Okay, I was looking at your files because I missed you two. There. Happy?"

Ed and Bo gazed back at Belfroy, and then slowly turned to each other. Ed's grin spread from cheek to cheek and Bo's spread even wider, if possible.

"Did he just say what he think I said?" Ed asked under his breath.

"He definitely just said what you thought he said."

"Anyways," Belfroy said, still grinning but slightly red for the first time. "I was looking through your files and came across the original count from the contest, the blind ballot we did."

Ed and Bo nodded, hearts thudding.

"And you two lost."

"We already knew that!" Ed exclaimed.

"Dude, if you wanted to rub it in, you didn't have to do all this shit first," Bo said dejectedly.

"No, listen to me, boys. You lost by a vote count of 3 to 2," Belfroy said with intensity, as if that information should resonate very strongly with the boys. They both stared back, unblinking.

"Okay, seriously, if you want to tell us exactly how and why we lost, we don't really care anymore," Ed began.

"I mean, we already told you we know all this stuff!" Bo yelled. The boys started to shuffle, tired of the repeated acknowledgement of their failures, when something incredible happened. Right in front of their very eyes, Belfroy's mouth began to twitch. His eyes watered slightly and the twitch grew. Before either of them could comprehend what was happening, Belfroy's carefully crafted smile crashed down into a thin straight line. The smile they had never seen him without was gone. In that moment, he looked like a robot that had just gained sentience. Ed and Bo both stopped talking and moving, because this was a sight that could not be unseen.

Belfroy leaned in close and spoke in a lowered tone the boys had never heard before. "There were only four judges," Belfroy said. "Ms. Jeralé, Principal Hunter, Paolo Müllers, and myself. And yet there were five votes."

"So someone added a fifth vote . . . " Bo said slowly.

"Without it, it would have been a tie," Ed theorized. Belfroy nodded.

"That's what I suspect."

"So what would have happened if we had tied?" Ed asked.

"We would have gone to an audience poll," Belfroy said. Bo shook his head and laughed.

"We would have won! The crowd was filled with our customers!"

Belfroy stared back at them. "Look, I don't have any proof here. But somehow, a vote was added and the person who counted the votes did not report the discrepancy."

They all sat in silence for a few moments. Ed

and Bo struggled to wrap their heads around what they had just been told.

"Who counted the votes?" Ed finally asked. Belfroy looked at both of them, and leaned in even closer.

"I'm glad you asked. The most impartial of us all. Paolo Müllers."

Now Ed and Bo needed to sit in silence for more than a few moments. They had no concept of what to do with this piece of information. Ed thought about the business trip Paolo had taken them on and the eventual deceit, and wondered how that could possibly connect to getting second place in the competition. Bo was still stuck on the fact that they definitely would have won if not for the extra vote, and had a feeling that things would have gone very differently for the two of them if they had become the winners of the competition.

When Hayley Plotinsky came back over to collect the bill, everyone jerked back to attention and Belfroy plastered his smile back over his face. She walked away with their cards in hand, and Belfroy looked at both Ed and Bo with his grin firmly affixed.

"I don't know what any of this means, but it means something," he said. "It means that you can't give up. It means that you have to beat Cameron. It means that this might be bigger than you may think."

Ed and Bo gulped and looked at each other, which is something they seemed to have a habit of doing in Belfroy's presence. Hayley avoided eye contact as she returned their cards, and Belfroy stiffly stood up.

"You can always reach out to me if you have any questions, and as always," he said without blinking, "hang in there."

Ed and Bo watched him leave, and then continued to stare after his exit, more than a bit dumbfounded. The wheels of something were in motion, but the boys could not exactly be sure what that something was.

"Pretty crazy, huh?" Bo asked when the silence had stretched too long for his comfort.

"Pretty crazy, indeed," Ed answered. He turned to Bo with a furrow in his brow. "But I don't know, man. I mean, yeah, maybe the competition was rigged somehow, but that doesn't really change anything, does it?"

"What do you mean?" Bo said with passion. "It changes everything!"

"Okay, yeah, I know how you think about these things," Ed began with a roll of his eyes. Bo had a somewhat annoying penchant for conspiracy theories, and once he started he was unable to stop.

"No, don't roll your eyes, dude. This is it. This is what I have been training for," Bo said with the twinkle in his eye that suggested an idea was dawning. "There is something going on and I think it might hold the key to getting the company back."

Ed looked back at him, feeling in his brain that they just needed to move on, but feeling in his heart that this could be one last adventure worth taking.

"What do you say, dude? Shall we win our company back?" Bo asked, his voice peaking nervously. Ed looked him up and down, holding the silence for a slightly uncomfortable amount of time. Bo squirmed a bit under the tension, and when he seemed like he couldn't take it anymore, Ed nodded quickly.

"Of course, man."

Bo sighed in relief and clutched his heart. "Don't you ever do that to me again."

Ed chucked a little guiltily. "Sorry. I couldn't resist."

"Well," Bo said, grasping the menu in front of him. "Shall we order?"

"Didn't we already order?" Ed asked.

"Uh . . . " Bo said, trailing off as he struggled to remember anything beyond the sheer shock of seeing Belfroy. "Well, even if we did, I could definitely eat again."

"Yeah, I guess I could too."

"Shall we?" Bo asked, gesturing widely to the plastic menu before them. Ed nodded.

"We shall."

By this point, they had been there for so long that Joseph's section had switched and he was now their waiter. When he approached them ten minutes later with a scowl on his face, Ed and Bo couldn't help but feel like they did something wrong.

"Didn't you guys already eat?" Joseph asked.

"We can't remember," Bo said. "But we would like to order again."

Joseph rolled his eyes and took their order. Ed and Bo both enjoyed their second meals—Ed had a chicken BLT with sweet potato fries and Bo had what may or may not have been his fourth milkshake of the day. They threw around theories for how exactly the votes to the contest had been rigged—ranging from Cameron bribing Paolo to it being Principal Hunter's plan the whole time to it maybe being due to aliens or at least robots. The more they talked, the less sure of themselves they were, and the less they knew what they should do next. When they came to the close of their second meal, they stared at each other in flat silence, feeling as if they had thoroughly exhausted all of their conspiracy theories.

Joseph, who had been walking in and out of their speculation, came over with the check and a deep furrow in his brow. The boys had been seeing a lot of furrowed brows these days and furrowing their own brows often as well, and they were starting to get sick of it. Joseph placed the check down at their table, and when Ed reached to pick it up, he paled instantly.

"What is it? Did they add an extra zero to the end of it? They can do that sometimes," Bo said. Ed shook his head, and Bo grabbed the check from him. Written in tiny font at the very bottom of the check was Joseph's scrawled text.

We are being watched. Meet me in the alleyway in 6 minutes.

Ed and Bo looked at each other, and then at Joseph, but he refused to make eye contact. They paid the second bill and tentatively made their way to alley.

Ed and Bo paced nervously in the alleyway behind Al's Diner. They were not nervous because they were in the alleyway—they had made many a purchase from Doug the Drug Dealer back here. They were nervous because this was starting to feel a hell of a lot like the French Mafia experience, and they had made a solemn pact to stay away from mafia affairs. Ed watched his watch anxiously, and Bo darted hopped from foot to foot. They felt like they were approaching Terror Town and they could see it in each other's eyes.

As they paced back and forth, a shrill screech reverberated out of the corner, and Ed jumped up, yelling in fear. This made Bo flinch and scream equally as loud. The boys felt the undeniable power of adrenaline course through their systems, and they prepared to defend themselves against certain attack. But instead of a scary intruder or a French newspaper gunman, a small rat scurried through the alleyway, chased by a slightly bigger rat. Bo immediately softened, but Ed jumped once more. Rats always made him uneasy.

"Dude, chill out," Bo said with a laugh. "It's just Ham and Cheese."

"You really need to stop naming every rodent in our lives," Ed grumbled.

"Well how else am I supposed to tell them apart when I talk about them?"

"Why do you need to talk about them in the first place?" Ed asked, but before Bo could retort, the door from Al's opened and the boys screamed once more. This time it was just Joseph.

"Dude!" Ed shouted.

"Dude!" Bo echoed. Joseph shushed them both.

"We have to be quick," he said. Ed and Bo both nodded, eyes wide and hearts thudding. Joseph pulled them into the corner from which Ham and Cheese had just erupted. Ed eyed the potentially rat-infested shadowy corner, but tentatively followed. Joseph dropped his head down low.

"Okay, guys. Listen. I was forced to leave Square One, and I had to sign a hell of a lot of contracts that forbade me from ever talking about anything that happened there," he said.

"Them and their contracts, am I right!" Bo said. "See, dude? Not just us," he said to Ed. Joseph shushed them once more.

"What I'm trying to say is that something big is happening."

"We know, we heard about the competition," Ed said.

Joseph looked back at them blankly and laughed. "Much bigger than some stupid high school competition." Just then, the sound of a car speeding by made all three of the boys jump. Joseph's eyes darted around the alleyway and he breathed a bit heavier.

"Okay. I have to go."

"But you didn't tell us anything!" Bo protested.

"What the hell happened when we were gone?" Ed asked.

Joseph had started toward the door, but turned around to look Ed and Bo in the eyes. "Okay. I'm going to tell you something I didn't tell Natalie."

Ed and Bo nodded, moving towards him.

"I overheard a conversation about names," Joseph said.

"We know that already!" Ed said, growing antsy with the repeated up and down swing of his heart cycles.

"Cameron was plotting the whole time to get our names taken off of the company, we know," Bo said.

"No," Joseph said. "There's more." He leaned in, and whispered, "It's all in the names."

With that, he turned around and headed resolutely back into the diner.

"Wait!" Ed shouted. "What does that mean?"

"Is that a metaphor?" Bo asked. "I'm very good at those usually but I don't understand this!"

Joseph was already halfway through the door. He stopped, his back to them.

"Sorry, that's all I can say." He turned around slowly, pain in his eyes. "They took all my hoodies, dudes."

With that, he was back in the diner, and Ed and Bo were left with the smell of trash and the faint squeaking of Ham and Cheese.

"We leave for a year and nobody makes sense anymore," Ed grumbled.

"Tell me about it," Bo said. "Maybe this is all just some big game or something. And Cameron is out there laughing his ass off."

"It's all in the names? That doesn't mean shit," Ed reiterated. The sun had set and with it, the promise of summer had set for the day as well. As the cooler air swept by them, the boys both shivered slightly. Ed sighed heavily. "Well. No use standing here with our backs up against the wall," he said. He turned to look at the wall behind them and chuckled. "Literally."

Bo nodded, and then abruptly stopped. "Wait. Ed. What did you just say?"

"Uh . . . No use standing here?"

"What else?"

"With our backs up against the wall?"

Bo nodded, and then nodded harder, and before long he was nodding so hard he looked like he was jumping up and down.

"Dude! What is it?" Ed yelled. Bo stopped abruptly and cackled. "That bastard thought he could fool us. He was so wrong."

"What do you mean?"

"I need a whiteboard and a marker and a lot of salt and vinegar chips and some weed, ASAP!" Bo yelled. He started to walk briskly out of the alleyway, leaving Ed staring after him.

"Where are you going?" Ed yelled.

"To your garage!" At that, he stopped in his tracks. "Oh. Right."

Ed shrugged. "We could go back to the rooftop?"

The thought of climbing that insurmountable

hill that their high school rested on top of exhausted Bo. Just when he was about to give up and sit down in the alleyway in defeat, a thought struck him. Bo turned around and looked Ed in the eyes.

"We could . . . go to my house?"

Ed felt the rules of his world crashing down around him. In all of their years of bestfriendom, he had never set foot in Bo's house. Not once.

"What?" Ed asked.

"I said that we could go to my house."

Ed looked at Bo and Bo looked back at Ed. This was the dawning of a new era, and the boys felt more than a little nervous.

"Okay," Ed finally answered.

"Okay?"

"Okay."

Bo nodded resolutely, and began to walk. Ed caught up with him, and the two headed down the street and toward Bo's house to figure out just exactly what was "bigger than all of them."

3

Ed and Bo stood outside of a very average looking house, as houses go. It was white with two stories, a basement, and a well-manicured lawn to round it out. They even had one of those "Bless This House" signs on the front door. Taken all together, it looked like every other house on the block, because it was like every other house on the block.

"What were you expecting?" Bo asked when he saw Ed's shocked face.

"I don't know. I think like either a tiny shack or a gigantic mansion or something at least a little weird."

Bo laughed. "You've never asked to come over!"

"Because you've never invited me!" Ed responded. Bo held the grocery bags filled with their supplies for higher thinking and shrugged.

"Maybe we're finally at that level of friendship."

He walked to the soft blue front door and Ed followed him. They crossed the threshold into a foyer, which was also as normal as could be expected. Carpeted stairs ran to the second floor, tiles faded from years of use covered the entryway, and the hallways extended in either direction. It was, in short, a house.

"Dude," Ed breathed out in awe. "This is, like, really a *house*."

Bo rolled his eyes and led Ed through the hallway on the left, past family pictures and Bo's drawings from grade school. Ed stopped to examine one or two of the family portraits—they featured a younger Bo, dressed entirely in white, with two people standing slightly behind him, dressed entirely in suits and dark sunglasses. Ed laughed out loud, but not for the reason Bo expected.

"I know. My hair was so weird then, huh?" Bo said.

Ed chuckled, but quickly stopped when he realized Bo was not kidding. Ed continued looking at the portraits on the wall, and saw framed pictures of the two people in suits in the background of various famous events, ranging from big pop concerts to the latest inauguration.

"Who are these people?" Ed asked.

"My parents," Bo said nonchalantly. Ed gestured at the pictures on the wall.

"Why were they at all this stuff?"

"Oh, just business travel," Bo responded. When Ed stared at him expectantly, Bo continued, sighing as if it should be obvious. "They work for the IRS."

Ed nodded, and suddenly Bo's government-fueled conspiracy theories took on a whole new light. They continued to walk through the labyrinth of hallways, and as Ed peered into each and every room he saw an eerie level of order and distinct lack of life. He touched the dining room table and felt a thin layer of dust. He wondered when exactly this place had last housed a family; from the looks of it, it had been quite a while. They paused at the threshold of the stairs leading into the dark basement, and Ed laughed nervously.

"Where are your parents, man?"

"At work. They're always at work. Those taxes don't do themselves, you know."

Ed was not one for conspiracy theories, but even he had to think that it didn't exactly seem like accountants lived in this house. But before he could voice any questions, Bo began to walk downstairs into the basement. Ed peered around the top floor once more before following his best friend into the depths of what may or may not be an FBI home-base. Bo cautiously walked down the stairs, and Ed cautiously followed him. Ed was utterly unsure of what he would find, and Bo was utterly unsure of how Ed would react. He finally got to the bottom of the stairs and flipped the switch, and Ed gasped.

"This is . . . "

"I know, I know, it's kind of weird," Bo said sheepishly as they looked around the room.

"No," Ed said with a growing smile. "It's amazing. Just like you did in New York!"

The room was decorated almost as exactly as Ed's garage had been, just as Bo had done at Square One headquarters in New York. Posters from various concerts Ed and Bo had attended stretched from wall to wall—apparently all those posters Ed had bought, Bo had bought a copy too. Each little trinket of memorabilia that had been in Ed's garage, Bo had one as well. He even had a dilapidated thrift store couch in the center of the basement, and though it was slightly greener, it was the thought that counted.

"How did you do this? When?" Ed asked incredulously. Bo shrugged.

"It's always made me feel like I was metaphorically *at home*, even when I was, like, literally here at home."

Ed felt like he was going to both laugh and cry at the same time, so all he could do was reach over and hug Bo, tightly but quickly. "This is awesome, dude," he said. When they broke apart, Bo looked a little ruffled as well, and it took turning on some music and breaking out their weed to relax the situation back to normalcy. Bo also had a convenient stash under his thrift-store couch, the same blue-strand they had smoked almost exactly a year earlier on Ed's birthday—back when Paolo had called them for the first time.

"Dude!" Ed exclaimed when he saw it.

"Dude. I know," Bo said sheepishly. "I couldn't stop myself from saving some of it."

Ed smiled wide, and took the bag of weed from him to attempt to roll a joint. He was still out of practice, and accordingly, it took him quite a bit of time to do so.

"You can, like, start your planning if you want to," Ed said, sweating a little under the strain of time-pressured rolling. "Don't wait for me."

"Nah, it's okay," Bo said, because truthfully he had mostly forgotten his earlier saving-the-day revelation and didn't want to admit it yet. Ed struggled with the joint for a couple more minutes before finally succeeding in one lumpy moderate success. He held it up high with honor, and Bo clapped appreciatively. They lit the joint, savoring the intense pineapple flavor and powerful kick of this strain. They settled deeper into the couch as the familiar roots grew.

After a few hours of cartoon watching, chip eating, philosophizing, and laughing, Ed suddenly remembered the intention of their visit.

"Shit! We totally came here for a whole brainstorming session thing!" he said.

"Oh," Bo said in a small voice, feeling Ed's expectant eyes on him, and utterly unable to recall anything beyond two minutes ago. "Maybe we should sleep on it."

"No way, dude! Let's do it! Let's take down Cameron! What's your inspiration?!"

Bo looked over at Ed and shrugged sheepishly. "I don't think I remember it anymore, man."

"Sure you do! It was something about . . . I said something about . . . and then you said that thing . . . "

He trailed off as they both became consumed by the struggle to collectively remember what had been said in the back alleyway. Truthfully, they could both only think about Ham and Cheese.

"Oh!" Bo finally said.

"Yeah! You got it!" Ed yelled back.

"It was totally something about . . . " Bo began, but then trailed off again. Both boys started to feel their pulse quicken in frustration; they were not as used to fleeting thoughts these days. Ed thought back to how good his brain had felt when he had studied for that Comp Sci Exam and gotten a B+, and Bo couldn't help but remember how clear his thoughts had been when he had been with Ted, gazing out at the mountainous regions before him. Back in their hazy, smoke-filled environment, their brains had slowed back down to their old speed. But then, as happened more often than not, inspiration struck Ed.

"I said, 'Backs up against the wall!'" he exclaimed, and that was all Bo needed.

"Oh, yes. Oh, man. Okay. We are ready." And with that, Bo jumped to his feet. He vaulted into the dusty corner of the back of the room, digging through skiing equipment, old helmets, and the like. Finally, he joyously pulled out his prize: a very tiny whiteboard. He turned to Ed with a broad smile, but Ed eyed the board suspiciously.

"That's the biggest size you have?"

"Dude," Bo responded. "This was all I needed when I was five."

He brought the whiteboard over to Ed, and sure enough, it was filled with crude stick-figure drawings and Bo's name. Bo smiled and wiped it off, flipping the board over in his hands to wipe off the opposite side. But when his eyes landed on the drawing on this side, his face fell into solemnity.

"What is it?" Ed asked. Bo just shook his head,

and turned the whiteboard toward Ed. The board was entirely covered with a map of the larger Portland area, complete with a dotted line that lead off through Washington, to the coast, and beyond. Underneath it, was the scribbled phrase: *Follow the line—you will find where he's been and the treasure will be within. Margaret.* Ed looked up at Bo in awe.

"This is just like . . . "

"That picture we found on your whiteboard," Bo finished. "But who is Margaret?"

Ed gazed back at Bo. "Margaret is my mother's name."

The boys sat in contemplative silence for more than a few minutes as this all sunk in. Back before the dawn of Square One, the two had unearthed a whiteboard in Ed's garage that contained a nearly identical map and message, except with Ed's father's signature.

"Where did you say your Mom was, again?" Bo asked.

"Uh, a business trip."

"But like, where exactly?"

"I'm not sure."

The silence washed over them once more. Ed sat up in his chair a bit straighter.

"How long have your parents been gone?" Ed asked.

"Three weeks. And your Mom?"

"Three weeks."

The boys gazed at the whiteboard, and Bo traced his finger along the dotted line. He didn't feel his internal conspiracy alarm sounding, but it seemed clear that something was not adding up. Ed let his eyes lose focus as he looked at the map. He had dreamt of more than one alternative fantasy as a child in which his father did not actually abandon them to escape gambling debt but was actually some sort of caped crusader or spy-pirate. But he was now an adult, and it was time to grow up. Bo looked at Ed, and Ed looked back. They both shrugged.

"Coincidence?" Bo asked.

"Coincidence," Ed confirmed. And with that, they erased the map and began their work. Unfortunately, the board was so small that Bo's sprawling font did not exactly fit coherently.

"What does that say?" Ed asked. Bo sighed, and held it just a bit closer to Ed's face. "I really cannot read that," Ed said.

Bo rolled his eyes and moved closer to Ed, until he was standing directly in front of Ed and holding the whiteboard directly in front of Ed's face. Ed squinted at it through his glasses, and finally shrugged.

"I don't get it."

Bo groaned, and turned the board back around. "What don't you get?" he asked impatiently.

"All you did was write a bunch of different names on there. Anybody could do that," Ed said. Bo shook his head and smiled at Ed more than a little patronizingly. He pointed to the first name he had written.

"Watloc, Inc. The competing delivery company

that made us sign Cameron's acquisition contract in the first place." He then pointed to the next name. "T.W. Alco. The French Mafia leader who almost destroyed us, as well as Dominique and Cléo, in France."

Ed furrowed his brow and narrowed his eyes, but these names meant nothing yet. Bo sighed heavily; for the first time he had figured out something before Ed and he wanted to make sure to rub it in.

"Cotlaw, Inc. The company that flew us out to California and tried to swindle us out of our ownership." Bo looked powerfully at Ed as he concluded, "Backs against the *wall*. Cameron *Wal*cot. Do you see what I mean?" he screeched. Ed stared at the tiny whiteboard for a long while, and finally, shook his head. Bo groaned.

"Sorry, dude," Ed said. "But all you're doing is naming stuff from our past! Are you sure this isn't more of like a dream thing instead of real life?"

Bo solemnly thought for a few moments. "I'll be right back."

Bo bolted upstairs, leaving Ed yelling after him. "Why don't you just explain it?" But Bo did not just want to simply explain something of this magnitude. No, this conspiracy theory deserved much more gravitas. Ed sighed, and opened another bag of salt and vinegar chips. The punch of vinegar overwhelmed him at first bite; his palate had adjusted to a diet distinctly lacking in salt and vinegar at school. But by the second and third chip, he remembered everything he had missed about the chips that used to be his way of life, and more.

Just as Ed was about to yell up the stairs that they didn't have time for this kind of theatrics, Bo came bounding back down, clutching something in his hands. He ran over to the outline of an old fridge that had not seen electricity or operation in many years, and plastered on an entire alphabet of magnetized letters. He looked back at Ed, smiling proudly.

"Uh, good job?" Ed offered. Bo turned back around to the fridge and busily rearranged. Ed sat back and munched on his chips, ready for another one of Bo's idea storms.

"Okay," Bo finally said, turning back around and presenting the fridge. "What does this say?"

Ed squinted, and read what he saw. "Walcot. Cameron's last name, I know, but what does that—" But Bo cut him off by holding up his hand. He moved the letters of Cameron's last name around and turned back.

"Now what does this say?" Bo asked.

Ed stared at it, taken aback, and then read aloud: "CotLaw."

Bo beamed. He rearranged the letters once more. "And now?" he asked.

"Watloc," Ed said, the fear in his voice rising. Ed rearranged faster.

"Now?"

"T.W. Alco," Ed said nervously.

"And now!" Bo said finally.

"Walcot," Ed breathed out in awe. Bo stared at

Ed, smiling resolutely. "It's all in the names, just like Joseph said. Literally," Bo said proudly.

Ed nodded and continued to stare breathlessly at the letters in front of him. He slowly rose to his feet and made his way over to the fridge, rearranging the letters and seeing for himself that they were all connected.

"It's an anagram," Ed declared. "They're all anagrams."

"I don't know what that is, but, yeah, maybe," Bo responded; he had given up his word-a-day calendar long ago. Bo slowly moved over to the couch and flopped down in exhaustion; this was the most alive conspiracy theory that he had ever encountered, and it was entirely overwhelming. After a few moments, Ed came down to the couch and sat down as well. They both sank deeper and deeper in to the floral couch, and finally, they turned to each other.

"So," Ed said.

"So," Bo answered.

"What does this mean?"

"I think this means that Cameron has been behind everything the whole time," Bo said. "I'm not exactly sure how, and I'm not exactly sure why. But this is most certainly *not* a coincidence."

Ed nodded slowly, and both boys sat eating chips for quite some time, struggling to wrap their minds around the evidence that they had just uncovered. Bo basked in his victory of figuring out the name clue for a while, until he remembered that there was still an incomprehensible array of other clues to uncover. Ed grappled with the fact that the friend he had trusted and believed in for so long had indeed been connected to the evils in their life since the very beginning. He had gone to Sunday School with Cameron, for Christ's sake. As long as Ed had known Cameron, he had known Cameron to be charming, effortless, and incredibly smart.

"This has to be some kind of huge misunderstanding," Ed said softly.

"Do you really believe that?" Bo asked.

Ed thought for a moment, and then shook his head. No, he knew in his heart of hearts and his mind of minds that Cameron was indeed the evil in their lives, but he needed some time to get used to the thought. When Bo looked over at Ed and saw the conflict awash over his face, his discovery glee softened just a bit. Sure, he had been right, but that meant that Ed had been wrong. Bo knew more than anyone how hard that could be to deal with; he was wrong at least six times a day. Bo reached over and grasped Ed on the shoulder, smiling in a way that tried to be comforting but ended up being kind of scary.

"Sorry, dude," Bo said. Ed nodded. The boys sat in contemplative silence for a few more moments, until Ed was driven to his feet by the overwhelming urge to do *something*, anything. He felt emotions bubbling up to the surface, and he wasn't exactly sure what to call them—they were a strange mixture of bad and good, scary and sad, thrilling and dangerous. Ed turned to Bo, the mixture of feelings manifesting as a dangerous glint in his eye, and started to speak fast. Very fast.

"Okay, so there's a plot and we have to first understand it before we can figure out how to take down Cameron and perhaps his entire family and win back our company and our fortune, so I guess the first step is," he paused as he erased Bo's tiny whiteboard and wrote on it, "Intel. We need to get it. We need to know it."

"Yeah!" Bo said, sitting upright and feeling propelled by the anxious energy of Ed. "I love intel, dude."

"Great," Ed said. "So how do we get it?"

Bo shrugged. As much as he loved the idea of intel, he was mostly entirely unsure how people went about getting it in real life. But as he looked around his basement, his eyes landed on one door that was always locked.

"Dude," Bo breathed out.

"Yeah?"

Once again, Bo bolted up the stairs with no

explanation. Ed shrugged and busied himself with more chips. A few minutes later, Bo returned with a key in hand and a smile on his face. He walked over to the door in the corner of the basement, and motioned for Ed to come with him.

"What is it?" Ed asked, staring at the nondescript door in front of them.

"My parents always keep it locked," Bo answered, and then turned to Ed with the same kind of glint in his eyes. "So, who knows?"

He slowly inserted the key and turned. Unfortunately, it was not the right key. Bo had grabbed one of many loose keys lying around in the kitchen, and of course, this one was not the one that would open the top secret basement door. Ed and Bo both traveled upstairs to conduct an extensive key search, one that produced many, many keys, but none of which opened the door. Just when they were about to give up, Bo remembered there was one place he had not checked. He found the spare set of house keys hanging on the key chain by the front door, and grabbed it. Bo stood in front of the door with Ed by his side, holding his breath as he tried the very last key option. To their shared amazement, the door slowly creaked open. Bo beamed at Ed, and Ed beamed back. They crossed the threshold into the dark room, and Bo switched the lights on.

Ed groaned. The room was entirely empty, a nondescript, white-walled box of a room. Hanging starkly on the back wall was a far too large portrait, archaically in the style of medieval artwork. Ed and Bo both gaped openly.

"Who the hell is that?" Ed asked. Bo shook his head.

"That's the Spooky Eye-Patch Hunchback of Grosvenor Street," Bo responded in a daze. Sure enough, the portrait featured the same squinting, crouched over, and grizzled old man whom Bo had once helped on a Square One call so many months ago. The Spooky Eye-Patch Hunchback, also known as Trevor, had told Bo a web of conspiracy theories about treasure and government cover-up and the like. He had even given Bo a map to give to Ed, which Ed had promptly thrown away.

"That dude that gave me that map?" Ed asked.

"The very same," Bo responded.

"Are you sure your parents are accountants?" Ed asked. The weird family portraits, the secret room, the framed picture of Spooky Eye-Patch Hunchback; it was all starting to feel like too much for workers who supposedly dealt with taxes. Bo peered at the label under the picture and read aloud, "*To Mr. and Mrs. Dawson. May my spirit watch over your endeavors even while I am in hiding. To everyone else: I am not hiding, so please do not come looking for me.*"

Bo turned back to Ed, his eyes wide. "Am I just really high or is this getting really bizarre?"

"Both."

Bo reached forward and started tapping on the portrait while Ed fell deeper and deeper into his contemplations. Maybe Bo's parents were involved with this treasure thing. Maybe the treasure thing was real. Maybe, just maybe, Ed's dad didn't leave them for Iowa. Ed was jolted out of his ruminations by a hollow thud as Bo tapped on the portrait. He turned to Ed and smiled.

"I saw this in a movie once," Bo said. "Also this is how my parents give me my Christmas present every year."

"What does it mean?" Ed asked, his pulse rising.

"It means that what we're looking for is behind here," Bo said. "You ready?"

"For what?" Ed screeched, but it was too late. Bo wound up his leg and administered a swift kick through the portrait. It instantly caved in, revealing an alcove within. Ed and Bo gazed at the multitude of platinum cases before them.

"What is it?" Ed asked breathlessly.

"It's how we're going to take down Cameron," Bo answered.

4

"**W**here the hell did you get all of this?!"
Natalie screeched. Ed and Bo looked at each other and shrugged.

"Bo's house," Ed answered.

"Bo's . . . *house?* You had him over to your house?" she said to Bo accusatorily. He shrugged sheepishly.

"You never asked!"

Natalie ran her hands over her shaved head and stared at the open cases before her.

"Well, I don't know if bringing all of this to the roof of your former high school was exactly the best idea," Natalie said.

"We didn't have anywhere else to bring them!" Ed said.

"And, it's a really nice day!" Bo added. Natalie looked back and forth between the two of them, and shrugged.

"So what's the plan?" she asked. "What the hell is all of this stuff for?"

"Uh," Bo said, trailing off. "That's what we hoped you would be able to help us with."

The trio stood in front the innumerable platinum cases Ed and Bo had transported from Bo's basement to the roof of I.M. High, a feat that was not easy by any means, but one that strangely seemed necessary at the time. The cases were filled with state of the art surveillance equipment, at least, that's what Ed and Bo assumed—everything was tiny and electronic and they were all kind of scared to touch it.

"I mean," Natalie said, gazing at the variety of tiny devices, "are there even any instructions or anything?"

Bo looked through the foam lining of one the cases and looked back up, shaking his head.

"Nope. But like, how hard can it be, am I right?" Bo reached into the case closest to him, which contained some sort of sunglasses. He touched the glasses, and they flipped of their own accord, landing back in the case. Everyone jumped back, emitting a few yelps of fear.

"Okay. Maybe it is a little hard," Bo admitted. Natalie surveyed the cases before them and the wild eyes of Ed and Bo, and smiled.

"I missed you guys," she said, and although her tone was a bit sarcastic, the boys could tell that she meant it. Bo and Natalie made eye contact once more, but before Bo could be transported back to the rush of feelings and emotions her eyes always sparked, he looked away. He reminded himself that avoiding the conversation about what they were "doing" for the rest of their lives wasn't exactly a sustainable plan, but he thought that it was at least a plan for now.

"Anyways," Natalie said, "let's break into the Walcot Mansion."

Ed laughed, and Bo laughed with him.

"What's funny?" Bo finally asked when Ed kept laughing.

"The Walcot Mansion is impenetrable, Natalie! Everyone knows that! When Tall Andres tried to TP his house in eighth grade, he got chased out by a pack of panthers," Ed said.

"Okay, first of all, it was definitely just attack dogs, not panthers," Natalie said.

"They love their large cats of prey!" Ed insisted.

"Secondly," Natalie continued, "no one else has ever had this platinum case bullshit, have they?"

Ed and Bo looked at the array of cases before them, and then back at Natalie.

"I don't have a better plan," Bo whispered under his breath to Ed.

"Me neither," Ed whispered back. Natalie smiled triumphantly.

"Let's break into the Walcot Mansion," Ed said with poorly restrained foreboding.

The trio spent the rest of the weekend doing their best to comprehend the variety of spy tools they had at their disposal. They lounged on the roof of their high school, reveling in the weekend calm the rooftop had to offer when school was not in session. They smoked whenever they lost inspiration, and ordered pizza whenever they got hungry. Each and every time they ordered pizza, they remarked how Square One should be the people delivering food, and that inspired them to keep going.

They found sunglasses that could see through walls if you pressed a tiny button at the bottom of the frame. They figured out how to use a smoke machine that could make them disappear at the touch of a button. They tested Tasers and stun guns on each other, and then decided that it was much safer to leave the weapons at home. They found a wiretap device, a device that made your shoes less squeaky, walkie-talkies, a pen that would also record audio, and a litany of objects that looked like normal office supplies but also probably had some other purposes too. They laughed and enjoyed themselves, but they also strangely stayed on task. Maybe it was maturity, or maybe it was just the need for revenge, but whatever the case, the group knew that they had to really apply themselves to defeat the evil mastermind known as Cameron Walcot. They grew more and more frustrated with the sound of the bulldozer, and they knew they needed to win their garage back.

When the weekend came to a close and Natalie had to finish all that homework she hadn't done, the boys discussed their plan over some desperately needed microwaved bagel bites, just like the good old days.

"Monday night is objectively the best night to conduct a covert operation," Bo stated.

"What about Tuesday?" Ed asked. "That's just like totally out of the blue. People are like, cooking and stuff on Tuesday nights."

"But they're so tired on Mondays!" Bo insisted. They continued to bicker for quite a while, until Bo won over Ed with his apparent spy-related expertise. After all, he did read quite a bit of mystery fan fiction in his day. They agreed on Monday, and by the time nightfall rolled around and they had exhausted their supply of microwaved food, the boys were collectively freaking out.

"How many panthers did you say there were?!" Bo asked frantically as they got dressed in Ed's room.

"At least seven," Ed answered solemnly. "This may be the last thing we ever do, dude. Just be prepared for that."

Bo gulped, because he still had a hell of a lot of other stuff he wanted to do, like confess his undying love to Natalie, for example. He pulled on his black t-shirt and turned to look at Ed. Ed looked back at Bo. They were both decked out in all-black attire and were quite lumpy from a variety of spy substances hidden at various points under their sleeves or in their pant legs or under their beanies.

"Dude," Ed said simply.

"Dude," Bo answered. They high fived. They had completely nailed it.

A few minutes later, Ed and Bo both anxiously paced in the kitchen, waiting for Natalie to finish her spy preparation.

"Hurry up!" Ed yelled up to Natalie. "We've got a house to break into!"

Natalie yelled something indistinguishable back, and Ed turned to Bo, eyes narrowed in annoyance. "Can you please go get her?"

Bo nodded and headed upstairs to Natalie's room, a place he had last been in the context of making out with her. He repeated to himself as he climbed the stairs that he could totally just be in her room like any normal friend of her brother's. After all, that's exactly what he was, at least until he made the eternal love confession. He tentatively knocked on the door, his breath catching in his chest.

"Just a second!" came her muffled voice from within.

"Okay," Bo said lamely. "Ed's just getting antsy."

A brief pause, and then Natalie opened the door slowly. "Hi."

"Hi," Bo responded. A long silence stretched between them, and then suddenly and without warning, Natalie was kissing Bo. Or maybe Bo was kissing Natalie, he was entirely unable to tell what came first. All he knew was that their tongues were suddenly touching, their lips were on each other, and it was as shocking as it was incredible. When they broke apart, Natalie exhaled heavily and nodded.

"Yeah, I needed that." With that, she shut the door, leaving Bo rooted to his spot and basking in her taste, an earthy, vaguely flowery taste he had just started to forget.

"I'll be down in a minute!" she yelled through the door. Bo nodded and tried to say something back, but was utterly unable to form anything beyond a cough. So he shuffled downstairs and splashed water on his face, mumbling nothing that made sense. Ed observed Bo's silence, flushed face, and dreamy expression, but did not say anything. He had discovered that it was best not to know certain details.

Finally, Natalie emerged in an all-dark, tight-fitting suit. Ed raised his eyebrows in disgust, whereas Bo distinctly tried to avoid staring and utterly failed.

"You're really going to wear . . . *that?*" Ed asked.

"Shut up," Natalie said. "It's the only all-black thing I own."

"It looks like a Catwoman costume," Ed remarked.

"It is."

"Oh."

They both looked to Bo as the one who often settled these issues, but Bo resolutely stared forward.

"Shall we?" Bo asked blankly, looking at the door. The group stopped bickering, gathered their gadgets, and headed to the Walcot Mansion. The walk through the dark suburban streets was tense and filled with nothing but silence. Each spy was very deeply lost in their own thoughts and fears of what lay ahead. They walked in silence, and they each prepared themselves for the end. Nobody was exactly confident in what the end entailed, but they knew it would come with a hell of a lot of drama.

They finally arrived outside of the majesty known as the Walcot Mansion, hearts beating fast with the anxiety of imminent spy operations. Spanning more acres than Ed and Bo could count on two hands were three basketball courts, two pools, one golf course, and four mini-golf courses. The estate was more than a little overwhelming. As they crouched in the bushes across the street and stared at the expanse before them, Bo saw dark shapes walking with the stealth of predatory success inside.

"I swear to god, that's a panther," he said.

"Why did you have to tell him that?" Natalie complained.

"Because it's true, Natalie!" Ed responded.

"Shhhh," Bo said, shushing them vehemently. "Look."

The trio turned their attention to the gate, which slowly started to swing open. They swiveled around to see a limo approaching the estate. The group cursed and ducked down as low as they could get.

"Do you think they saw us?" Ed asked frantically.

"Almost definitely," Natalie responded.

Bo frantically fumbled with an object in his belt and then, without warning, a cloud of smoke exploded over all of them.

"What the hell was that for?" Ed coughed, jumping up and trying to do his best to breathe. Natalie shielded her face and Bo choked as smoke encompassed his mouth and eyes.

"Now they won't see us!" He coughed.

"Yeah, but they'll see a huge cloud of smoke!" said Natalie.

"Oh," Bo said. "I guess I didn't think about that."

The group slowly army-crawled across the dirt,

dragging themselves away from the conspicuous smoke bomb and inching toward fresh air as best as they could. When they finally resurfaced from the cloud of smoke, gasping for air, they all turned their attention back to the mansion. From this distance, it was impossible to tell, but what very closely resembled the figure of Cameron stepped out of a limo and walked into the house. Before they could see anything else, the front gate shut with a resounding clang, leaving the trio just where they started. Well, technically, a few yards away from where they had started.

Ed, Bo, and Natalie all looked at each other with wide eyes.

"He's home," Ed said, and everyone nodded. They all sat silently, absorbing the fact that they would soon be breaking into the Walcot Mansion, potentially fending off seven panthers, and facing Cameron himself. Bo cleared his throat.

"Are you all ready?"

Ed and Natalie both nodded. Bo held out his

hand. First Ed put his hand out, and then Natalie. They looked around at each other, and Bo whispered, "For Square One!" They raised their hands up, but not high enough to be detected, and then began to scale the garden wall.

It proved to be much harder than it looked. Ed had declared that the garden wall was absolutely the best way to enter, but then again, the last time he had been over at the Walcot Mansion, he had been eight and the garden wall had been built twice as tall since then. After a variety of unsuccessful attempts from all the operatives involved, Natalie held out one of the many spy tools: a rope attached to a grappling hook. She threw it over the wall and painstakingly scaled up, finally reaching the top and jumping down to the other side. For a few tense moments, the boys heard nothing.

"Natalie? Natalie!" Bo whispered urgently. Then finally, a soft murmur.

"I'm safe. No panthers." Bo breathed a sigh of relief and went next, although his ascent was much less graceful. He had the muscle power to get to the top, but also had a complete lack of flexibility or awareness of how to use the muscle power. After more than a few minutes, he plunged down to the other side as well without much control. While Ed grunted and huffed his way to the top of the wall, Natalie and Bo did the most sensible thing possible and made out, lost in each other's lips, faces, tongues, and hair or lack thereof once more. They broke apart just in time to see Ed falling down to the ground next to them with a dull thud. Bo was starting to think that he could get used to this whole spy business.

They creeped as silently as they could around the side of the sprawling mansion to attempt to break in through the door reserved for deliveries and the maid service. They stood outside the non-descript door in the faint shadows of distant street lamps, bickering about the best way to get in.

"I'm telling you," Bo whispered as he dug through his shirt. "I have some sort of lock pick in here somewhere."

"We don't need a lock pick when we have rocks!" Natalie insisted, holding up a medium-sized rock she had found on the ground. Ed continued to shush them and held out his screwdriver.

"We just have to unscrew the door handle, and then we are in!"

They fumbled with their tools, their words, and each other, and so didn't even notice when the door opened.

"Hello?" Mr. Walcot said, squinting into the dark. Ed, Bo, and Natalie froze. "Who's there?"

Bo slowly reached for his smoke bomb, and then cursed himself for setting it off earlier. Mr. Walcot stood in the doorway. He was tall, well-built, and well dressed in a tailored gray suit. He held a bag of trash in one hand and a cell phone in the other.

"What are you doing here? I'll call the cops!"

Ed was the first to step forward, clearing his throat awkwardly. "We just, uh, came to say, 'Hey!' I'm a friend of Cameron's," he said in a pitch that was not at all convincing.

"Then, why do you have a screwdriver?" Mr. Walcot asked quizzically.

"It's for uh, uh . . . " Ed trailed off, looking for help from Bo.

"We came to fix your windows!" Bo said. Ed shot him a look, and Bo shrugged.

"Just your regular window-fixers," Natalie said pleasantly. Mr. Walcot eyed them up and down with narrow eyes.

"You better get out of here," he said. "I know who you are."

"If we could just talk to your son first," Ed began, but Mr. Walcot cut him off with the raise of his hand.

"He doesn't want to talk to you. Now please leave before it's too late."

Ed, Bo, and Natalie stood on the threshold of the Walcot Mansion, but remained futilely unable to enter. They hesitated for just long enough to see Mr. Walcot's frown falter.

"Please leave now!" he repeated, and as the group

finally started to leave, Mr. Walcot mouthed something almost entirely indistinguishable.

"What?" Bo shouted, and Mr. Walcot mouthed it again. All three of them tried to grasp what he was saying, but the shadows cast a lot of doubt on and around his mouth.

"One more time!" Ed yelled. But when they heard the voice of Cameron echo through the hallway, "Is someone there, Dad?" Mr. Walcot closed the door in a hurry. Ed, Bo, and Natalie turned around and ran, clambering over the wall and falling to the ground on the other side. They ran all the way back to the DeLancey's house, and did not stop until they were safely behind a locked door. They did not even stop to say hello to Four. They stood and looked at each other, huffing and out of breath almost entirely.

"Did anyone see what Mr. Walcot said?" Bo asked. "It looked like, 'Cheese Fray Thee' to me, but that doesn't make sense."

"I saw, 'Trees Lay Here,'" Ed offered. They

turned to Natalie, who was flushed from running and pale from what she had seen.

"I think he said, 'Please Save Me,'" she said softly. Ed and Bo looked back at Natalie. They all felt a collective chill run down their spines, and they had no idea what to do next.

"What now?" Bo asked.

"I don't know," Natalie responded.

"Me neither," Ed said.

The trio stood in the kitchen for quite some time, and as the structure of the world they knew caved in around them, Ed couldn't help but think of his repeated stress dream, the one in which he was running and the ground was falling. Then an idea struck him.

"We need to call in back up," Ed said.

5

Ed and Bo sat at an exposed brick table in the RedElephant, nervously sipping their coffees. Well, Ed was nervously sipping his. Bo had ordered several espressos, against Ed's advice, and had already downed three cups in the French manner. Bo sat, jittery and wired, literally bouncing up and down in his seat. Ed continued to scan the room, waiting for their guest.

"Where the hell is she?" Bo said, his voice uncontrollably loud.

"Dude. For the last time. It is not okay to drink that much espresso," Ed said, taking a stress bite out of his chocolate croissant.

"It's how the French do it!" Bo yelled back. This was of course, not true, but Ed did not have the mental space to argue with him. Instead, he checked for the sixtieth time that their guest was not already seated amongst the city's hippest. RedElephant housed the area's best coffee, and its rustic décor ensured that it was always filled with the trendiest Portland had to offer. Once they had even seen Belfroy here, sporting his beret and trying to fit in as best he could. When they had imagined signing with CotLaw a year ago, they had envisioned holding business meetings in this very coffee shop. Ed thought it a little ironic that they were now meeting in the same shop to discuss the death of their business. He tried to get Bo's attention to communicate that sentiment, but Bo's eyes were wandering across the entire room and he seemed one sip of espresso away from sprinting out the door. Ed sighed, and handed Bo a glass of water so that he wouldn't get too dehydrated.

"Do I look okay?" Bo asked, gesturing to his

coffee-stained t-shirt and askew man-bun. Ed laughed and shrugged.

"You look fine. Do I look okay?"

Bo eyed Ed's disheveled t-shirt and very visible sweat marks and nodded whole-heartedly. This was Ed's signature non-suit look.

"Are you nervous?" Bo asked. His heart was thudding beyond control.

"A little," Ed admitted. "But mostly excited."

"I'm so nervous. Or maybe it's just all the caffeine. It's kind of hard to tell after a while, you know?"

Ed nodded. Every time Bo drank this much coffee he expressed these same sentiments. Bo reached for the croissant and took it out of Ed's hands, finishing it in one big bite.

"Hey!" Ed exclaimed.

"What?" Bo asked. His mind was already elsewhere. Just when Ed was about to force Bo to buy a replacement croissant, the woman they had been waiting for walked through the door. Bo gasped, and Ed turned around and smiled broadly. In the doorway, Rosalie Müllers removed her glasses and revealed the fiery eyes beneath. She scanned the room, eyes passing over the myriad of young cool kids, before landing on the two distinctly uncool kids sitting in the corner of the back room. She smiled and waved. They waved back.

"Okay, be cool, be cool, be cool be cool," Bo whispered under his breath.

"I am cool! You be cool!" Ed whispered back. They looked up just in time to smile pleasantly at Rosalie.

"Hello!" she said joyously. Her voice was as sharp as they had remembered it, but the locks of hair draping across her shoulders softened her face. Instead of the business attire they had always seen her in, she sported jeans and a hoodie. She still emitted the same sort of confident, intoxicating aura that immediately made the boys swoon. They both lurched to their feet awkwardly, and Bo tripped slightly in his excitement to stand up. They leaned in for hugs at varying speeds, which ended up resulting in a giant mess of limbs bumping and everyone awkwardly chuckling at the same time. They broke apart, and Rosalie laughed.

"You boys have changed," she said softly, even though that's precisely how they had said goodbye so many months ago. She sat down authoritatively.

"How can you tell?" Ed asked, a blush spreading across his face.

"I just can," she said. Bo bounced in his seat, overwhelmed by his beating heart.

"Can I get you anything to drink? They have great espresso here," he said. "Also the iced chais are great and the lattes and there's almond milk and the croissants are amazing and—"

Rosalie reached out and pulled Bo down, laughing as she did so. "Sit down, please. You're making me nervous."

"He has a way of doing that," Ed said with a smile. She looked back and forth between the two boys, and both of them blushed in turn. It seemed as if it would take quite a while to adjust to Rosalie's aura.

"So," Rosalie said after many moments of silence. "What would you boys like to talk about?"

They both peered back at her, their brains momentarily clouded by all-consuming excitement.

"How have you been?" Bo asked when the silence had stretched too long and they still needed to buy some thinking time.

"I've been great," she said, and her eyes let them know she was telling the truth. "I quit after that Forbes article on you two. Well, actually, 'fired' might be more accurate. Let's just say it was a mutual decision," she said with a laugh. "And I've been working as a freelance journalist ever since. It's been incredible," she concluded. "And you two? Last I saw Square One was taking over the market."

"Well," Ed said hesitantly. "That's sort of why we need to talk to you."

"We've been duped," Bo said blankly. "Again.

And we need to double-dupe or something in order to get our business back."

Rosalie nodded, looking back and forth between the two of them. "Was it Cameron?"

Ed and Bo both exclaimed.

"You knew?" Ed asked incredulously. Rosalie shrugged.

"I had some strong suspicions."

"I guess we were wondering what exactly you know about Mr. Savage and Cameron Walcot," Bo said. Rosalie looked back and forth between the two of them and breathed a heavy sigh. "How much time do you have?" she asked.

"We don't have jobs anymore," Ed barked out in a laugh.

"So, all the time you need," Bo finished. Rosalie nodded, and took out the same pad of paper she had used once upon a time to compile all those research notes on them.

"Well, to start with, Paolo is not actually my cousin," she said. Ed and Bo stared back at her.

"He's not?" was all Bo could muster. Rosalie shook her head. "Mr. Savage thought that it would be a good idea to present a duo in charge of dealing with you two. Which leads me to the next thing—I did not work at CotLaw until a few weeks before you two came in."

When they looked at her without comprehension, she continued. "They hired me exclusively so I could trick you guys into signing the contract."

Ed and Bo nodded; this was surprising, but not all that surprising, considering the overwhelming deceit they had grown used to dealing with.

"What do you know about Mr. Savage?" Ed asked once more. He had thought that the business guru himself could maybe be a part of the key to discovering this mystery.

"I don't think he exists," Rosalie said. "I'm pretty sure he's Cameron, or someone working for Cameron. The entire time I worked for CotLaw, I never once saw Mr. Savage in person. He only ever phone conferenced, and his voice always sounded terribly, suspiciously young."

Ed and Bo nodded, and Rosalie looked back down at her notepad. "And let's see, well, as you know, Cameron won first place in the Young Rising Entrepreneur Competition, but the strange thing is, as far as I know, there was never a meeting between Mr. Savage and Cameron."

"Which was the prize of the competition," Ed said thoughtfully.

"Exactly. I checked into the scheduling records on file at CotLaw and could not find a single reference to Cameron Walcot."

"So how do you know anything about him being involved, then?" Bo asked.

"Well," Rosalie said, leaning in. "Here's where it gets interesting. After Mr. Savage had one of his conferences with Paolo—he was allowed to speak to him whereas I was eternally shut out—anyways, I used the CotLaw reception phone to redial the number that had just called."

Ed and Bo stared at her as she took a dramatic pause.

"And?" Bo finally said, hanging onto her every word. She smiled and leaned in. "And. Guess who picked up?" After a few beats, she answered her own question. "Cameron Walcot."

Ed and Bo gasped right on cue, and Rosalie smiled at them. "That's what made me do all this digging on this Cameron guy in the first place. And I found more. Mr. Savage has never had a public appearance in all of his years of running CotLaw. I also strongly suspect that all the workers in the CotLaw headquarters may have been actors— nobody really knows what CotLaw does. They all looked cool and relaxed because they were literally never doing any work. I don't know what's going on, but I know it's something shady," she finished breathlessly. A few beats of silence stretched between them, and Rosalie averted her eyes.

"But in all of my research, I still have one question I can't answer," she continued. "Where does the Walcot fortune come from? It might be impossible to find out," she said softly.

"Wow," was all Ed could muster this time.

"Dude," Bo breathed out. Rosalie looked back and forth between them, and nodded.

"There's one more thing," she said softly. "I'm— uh. I'm sorry about what happened. I really regret my part in all of it. You two don't deserve that. You're just kids, and you lost a year of your childhood."

Ed and Bo looked back at her and laughed. "Are you kidding me?" Bo asked. "You wrote that article about us that catapulted us to fame! We couldn't have done it without you!"

"And also we are *not* kids," Ed said with his shoulders held squarely.

"Well, actually . . . " Rosalie said, her lips thinning. Ed and Bo eyed her warily. "It wasn't exactly my idea to write that article," Rosalie said, looking down at her hands.

"Then who's was it?" Ed asked tentatively.

"Mr. Savage's. He set up the deal and the publication and all that. It was the last thing I did before I quit," Rosalie said.

Ed and Bo looked at each other, both a bit paler than before.

"Oh," Bo said.

"I see," said Ed.

"It doesn't mean that anything I wrote in that article wasn't true!" she said quickly. "I stand behind everything in there."

Ed and Bo both nodded blankly.

"But what this means is that Cameron was behind the article," Ed said slowly.

Rosalie looked at the two of them grimly. "Maybe."

Ed and Bo didn't exactly feel like drinking coffee anymore.

The boys slowly walked through the streets of their neighborhood, too exhausted even to smoke.

"Dude. He's a genius," Bo said as he kicked a rock while he walked.

"He's orchestrated this whole thing," Ed agreed.

Bo took out the whiteboard that he had brought with him for emergency brainstorming, and began to write in incredibly small handwriting: *Step one: he rigged the contest.*

"So, when we lost, we were bummed. But when Paolo approached us about working together, we were so psyched, we said yes without really reading the contract," Ed reasoned.

Bo nodded and wrote, *Step two: he tried to get Paolo and Rosalie to convince us to sell the company.*

"Step three," Ed said. "He had Rosalie write that article when that failed, which led to our fame and the French trip."

"And T.W. Alco," Bo said. "But where does the Walcot fortune come in? Who is Cameron controlling? Are they all Cameron, or his relatives, or what?!" He suddenly stopped in his tracks and threw the whiteboard to the ground angrily. "It's too confusing!" he yelled loudly. "And I don't care about what any of it means. We're never going to take Cameron down."

Ed turned to him and bent down to pick up the whiteboard. "I don't know, dude. Maybe you're right. Maybe we should stop."

Bo shrugged. "Better to quit while we still have our dignity." When Ed looked away, Bo struggled to keep his face contorted into a frown.

Ed did not respond for quite a while, but thought that maybe Bo was right. He thought about all the time he had wasted on the company and how he had nothing to show for it, now. He fell deeply into his morbid contemplations, and didn't even notice when they had arrived at Ed's house. They stood outside the front door, and Ed looked at Bo with despair written across his face.

"What do we do, man?" Ed asked. Bo couldn't contain himself anymore; his smile spread openly. "How can you smile at a time like this?" Ed asked. "Our world is crumbling down around us."

"I called in back up," Bo said smugly.

"I know," Ed said wearily. "We already met with Rosalie, and she kind of made things worse."

"No," Bo said. "I called in other back up."

Ed looked at Bo in confusion, then to the front door. Bo motioned for him to go inside, and so Ed stepped toward the door and hesitantly opened it.

"'Ello," uttered the voice that Ed had been hearing in his dreams ever since he had left France. He stood dumbstruck as he looked back at the wide eyes and stern smile of the only woman he had ever truly loved. He also was not aware that he had loved Cléo until this moment, when he saw her again. Her hair was cut stylishly short, a style that he had mocked on his sister but seemed to make Cléo even more beautiful, if that was possible. Her freckled face was almost overrun with the near-summer speckles, and her loose clothing suggested she had been traveling for quite some time.

Next to her stood Dominique, tall and as constant as ever; a wild mane of hair stretched above her head and seemed to be larger than her. She shouted a kind, *"Bonjour,"* that carried across the room with jubilance. Bo bounded forward and hugged first Dominique, his spiritual counterpart, and then Cléo, with ease. He grinned from ear to ear and excitedly chattered with the two of them.

Meanwhile, Ed stood rooted to his spot. He couldn't stop staring at Cléo and was intimately struggling to tell if this was a dream or not. Sure, today had felt a lot more real than most of his dreams, but then again, his dreams usually always ended with seeing Cléo. He looked around nervously for a red-tailed hawk, Cléo's symbol and the signature of any good dream. But then she looked at him and slightly relaxed her thin frown into a near-smile, and Ed knew that this had to be real. He slowly crossed the foyer toward her, locked in eye contact the entire time. Bo watched the slow movement unfold, and pulled Dominique aside. They watched from the dining room as Ed inched slower and slower toward Cléo.

"What is going to happen?" Dominique asked with concern. Bo laughed.

"I have no clue."

Ed continued to inch closer, and Bo held his breath.

"She likes him quite a bit," Dominique said simply.

"He dreams about her every night," Bo responded. "I caught him just staring at pictures of red-tailed hawks the other day." They both peered around the edge of the doorframe as Ed and Cléo finally reached each other. But, bizarrely, neither of the two potential lovers moved.

"What the hell are they doing?" Dominique asked.

Ed and Cléo were merely standing a few inches from each other in utter silence. No hugging, no kissing, no talking. Cléo stared into Ed's eyes and Ed stared back.

"I'm a little concerned," Bo whispered when this had gone on for quite some time.

"Should we stop watching?" Dominique asked.

"If this is wrong then—"

"We don't want to be right," Dominique concluded.

So, they continued to watch as Ed and Cléo stared at each other in silence. Finally, after what seemed to be a lifetime, Ed found the words he needed to say.

"I think I'm in love with you," he said brazenly. Cléo rolled her eyes with a familiar glare.

"Shut up," she said. So he did. They stared at each other for a few more moments, and then she reached forward and grabbed Ed's thin body, pulling him close. He found his arms wrapping themselves around her, and he unfamiliarly held her into his chest. He noticed for the first time just how little she was.

Dominique and Bo started to think that maybe they were indeed witnessing a private moment, so they slowly tried to inch away. But, Bo was so focused on not missing a single moment of spying that he tripped over his feet and came tumbling to the ground in the dining room. The resulting sounds viscerally jerked Ed and Cléo away from each other. They curtly nodded, and slowly made their way over to Dominique and Bo.

"That was very weird," Dominique whispered to Bo as she saw them approaching.

"Ed's a weird dude," Bo answered, reddened from the fall.

Soon enough, the four of them were all standing together in Bo's kitchen, chattering and loudly catching up on their lives apart. Dominique and Cléo had been living in Sweden for almost a year, and found the culture to be quite blonde. They had been living and working on a French-speaking farm, and had decided that it was a relief to get out of the tech business for a while, and an even bigger relief to get out of the Mafia business.

"Which brings us to why we are here," Cléo said simply. "You need our help to defeat the American arm of the French Mafia."

Ed and Bo looked at each other, laughing at the misunderstanding.

"Oh no," Bo said, "you must have misheard me. We need your help to defeat Cameron Walcot."

This time Dominique and Cléo were the ones to look at each other pointedly. They turned back to the boys with grim smiles fastened to their faces.

"We are speaking of the same entities," Cléo said grimly. Ed and Bo felt the pits of their stomach drop even further, because as they had repeatedly been told, this was far bigger than they had ever expected.

"**W**ell, hello!" Natalie exclaimed. "If it isn't the woman Ed has told me *so* much about," she said as she grasped Cléo in a firm hug. Cléo looked over Natalie's shoulder to Dominique, eyes wide. Nobody had ever approached Cléo with such familiarity. Ed felt his pulse quicken and had a growing urge to lock Natalie in the acquisitioned garage.

"Okay, Natalie, that's more than enough," Ed said, trying to laugh and pretend everything was cool. But Natalie kept Cléo trapped in her strong embrace, speaking as she did so.

"It is. Such. A. Pleasure. I've waited my whole

life to meet someone crazy enough to like Ed, and well, he had to leave the country to find that!"

Cléo started to pale due to lack of oxygen, and Natalie finally released her.

"Let's go to my room. We have so much to catch up on," Natalie said, grabbing Cléo by the arm and taking her towards the stairs. Ed stepped firmly in her way, laughing once more and trying his hardest to appear calm.

"Okay, Natalie. Really. That is enough."

Natalie ignored him, walking directly past him and dragging Cléo with her. "Dominique, you can come too!" she yelled over her shoulder. As she turned around, she made eye contact with Ed and glared with the triumph of a little sister who finally had the chance to repay some of the damage her brother had done over the years. Dominique shrugged and stepped past Ed, and the three women left the two boys staring after them at the foot of the stairs.

Ed angrily turned to face Bo, eyes blazing.

"Why the hell did you let that happen?"

Bo just shook his head and smiled. "Dude. I don't understand them anymore than you do."

"Well," Ed said, still staring up the stairs with obvious worry, "what do we do now?"

"I guess we wait for them to come down," Bo said. The boys slowly sat down at the dining room table. Ed held his head in his hands, and Bo stared off into space. When Ed harrumphed for the sixth time, Bo stood up and retrieved the emergency stash of kitchen weed from under the sink. He brought it back to Ed, who nodded aggressively.

"Please."

As they packed a bowl using their old orange piece, Ed detailed how and why Natalie was a terrible sister and person in general, and finally, Bo couldn't take it any longer.

"Okay, dude, calm down," Bo said as he lit the piece for Ed.

"I am calm!"

"No, you're not, and you do this shit to Natalie all the time," Bo said.

"Okay, I don't really need this from you," Ed answered. He held out the piece to Bo, and Bo grabbed it.

"No, maybe you do," Bo said, the thoughts spilling out of his head. "You're so terrible to the dudes Natalie dates, we had to hide it from you, for like a long time, dude. I mean, I'm your best friend, and even *I* was afraid to tell you, and then it tore our friendship apart for . . . a long time. That's not a good thing."

Ed looked at Bo with surprise. This was unchartered territory.

"Part of why New York sucked so much for me was having to lie to you all the time, dude. Maybe it's time you realize that your sister is grown up."

Bo let out a long stream of smoke, and handed the piece back over to Ed. They smoked in stony silence for longer than usual, until Albert the cat sprinted around the house in pursuit of what appeared to be a mouse. Ed jumped up and yelled, Bo sneezed due to his cat allergy, and they both laughed.

"I forgot about that cat," Bo said warily, wiping his now-tearing eyes. "I preferred the Alberts in New York, to be honest." Their street-friend, Crazy Pigeon Man, had controlled at least nine pigeons, each of which was named Albert.

"Well, yeah, he named those pigeons after the original Albert," Ed said.

"I thought he named the pigeons after himself?" Bo asked. Crazy Pigeon Man had also responded to Albert along with each of his pigeons.

"Yeah, obviously, *all* of them are named after my cat," Ed said, as if that should be obvious. "Especially Crazy Pigeon Man."

"I don't think that's possible," Bo said with a laugh.

"Hey," Ed said, lowering his voice, "Albert gets around. He does a lot more than people give him credit for." It had now been almost a year since Ed had started to believe that Albert the cat potentially had the power of speech, and so he was not at all alarmed when Crazy Pigeon Man had told him who his true namesake was. "Anyways," Ed said, shaking himself out of his cat-fueled conspiracy. "I can't believe we have another goddamn mouse here!"

"Oh. Yeah. That's Andrew."

"Andrew?"

"Andrew."

"You *really* have to stop naming our mice."

The boys jumped up and chased Albert and Andrew out the front door, giggling as they did so. The brief confrontation of a few minutes prior was long forgotten, and even longer forgotten when they landed at the feet of the grim security guard, Four.

"Uh, hi," Bo said tentatively. Four nodded his hello.

"How . . . are you?" Ed asked. Four shrugged.

Bo slowly extended the orange piece that still had a few buds remaining.

"Do you . . . smoke?"

Four eyed the piece eagerly. "I'm not supposed to while I'm on duty."

"But you're always on duty!" Ed exclaimed.

"Exactly."

A few puffs of steam rose from the tip of the still burning weed, and Four's nostrils flared wide. His eyes darted left, and then right.

"Okay, maybe just one hit," Four said. He tentatively accepted the orange piece and inhaled deeply, and Ed and Bo both grinned.

A few hours later, Dominique, Cléo, and Natalie emerged from Natalie's room, full of smiles, shared stories, and inside jokes, to find the boys sitting in a circle with Four. They all seemed to be getting endless enjoyment out of rolling a tennis ball across the ground to each other.

"What is . . . this?" Natalie said with alarm

coloring her voice. Ed and Bo grinned back at her hazily.

"This is Freddie!" Bo said, gesturing to the security guard.

"Your nametag says . . . 'Four,'" Dominique said flatly. Freddie's face immediately fell. "That's what my official name is," he said. His grim demeanor returned, and he shakily stood up to resume his post, kicking the tennis ball away as he did so. "Move along now," he said sternly. Ed and Bo gazed up at him, unable to comprehend the Freddie to Four switch.

"But Freddie—" Bo began.

"Move. Along," he responded. Natalie guided the two boys away from the garage, and Dominique put a comforting hand on their backs.

"It is okay," she said. "He simply has lost his identity in the mass of consumerism known as the Walcot Foundation. It happens to the best of us."

Ed and Bo wearily shrugged, as they were both tired of losing people's identities to Cameron

Walcot. Dominique, Cléo, and Natalie began to walk down the driveway in line, and after a few moments, Ed and Bo realized that they should follow. The women led the boys down the street and toward town.

"Where are we going?" Bo asked when the thought struck him. Cléo grimly smiled.

"The library."

Bo's heart thudded in his chest, and he looked over to Ed. Ed grimly looked down at his feet.

The group stood outside of expansive gray building known as the "Public Library." Bo shuddered.

"I never thought we would have to step foot inside one of these," he said.

"Oh yeah! Man! I have never been inside a library ever!" Ed yelled in an effort to cover the fact that he had indeed been inside a library, and quite often during his academic career. Bo gazed at Ed suspiciously.

"Oh my god," he said after a few moments of study. "You totally went inside a library when you were at school, didn't you!"

"What?!" screeched Ed. "Uh, nah, of course not." When Bo continued to stare back at him, Ed caved. "Okay, yeah, like only because they are actually really great places to get information and study!"

"Dude," Bo breathed. "It's like I don't even know you anymore."

They didn't have time to keep discussing the betrayal of entering a library, because Cléo charged forth, with Natalie and Dominique closely in tow. Ed followed next, and then Bo, with heavy feet. Their neighborhood's public library was just as could be expected to any person who had ever been inside a library before, but to Bo, it was a whole new world.

"What's that smell?" he asked in wonder as they stepped through the front doors.

"Books, dude," Ed answered.

"It's incredible."

The library was lined with shelves, brightly colored labels, and various displays, and it was almost too much for a library newbie like Bo. Cléo marched with haste to the front desk and rang the bell for a librarian.

"'Ello! 'Ello?!" she yelled. It echoed through the library, and everybody in the group shushed her, except Bo, who didn't really know proper library etiquette yet. Soon enough, a short-haired and wiry woman came bounding over, one whom Ed and Bo had spent a lot of time with back in the day.

"Hello, how can I help you today—Ed? Bo?"

"Miss Dina!" Ed and Bo both cried at the same time, and then turned to each other in a flurry.

"Oh no," Cléo whispered.

"Not again," Natalie said.

"This will be embarrassing," Dominique said.

"Jinx!" the boys both yelled. As they ran around the library overturning trash cans and searching for any form of soda, Natalie looked to Miss Dina with an apology in her eyes.

"Can we get a study room?"

A few sodas and a few near-expulsions from the library later, the group stood around an adequately sized whiteboard in one of the library's small study rooms.

"So," Natalie said.

"Yes," Cléo answered.

"What?" Bo asked.

"This soda tastes terrible," Ed said. Bo sulked in the corner.

"Sucks for you for finding diet," Bo said with attitude.

"Why are we in this tiny room?" Dominique asked.

They were all standing in front of the blank whiteboard and everyone generally felt confused. Cléo yelled for order and everyone turned to her. She held up a marker.

"This is why we are here," she said. "We hear this is how you work."

Ed and Bo looked at each other, and then at Cléo. They shrugged.

"I mean, like sometimes, I guess," Bo said.

"But we also just like say stuff a lot," Ed added. Natalie groaned, and made a motion that the boys didn't catch, but it sent Dominique and Cléo into hysterics. Ed moved forward and grabbed the marker with energy, turning to the whiteboard before him.

"Seems like we also could have done this at home," Ed grumbled as he started to write on the board. Natalie sighed heavily and made another face.

"We're also here to do research, dude," she said. "Everyone ready?"

The people in the room looked around at each other, and nodded. They were as ready as they could be. For the next few hours, or maybe it was more—everyone lost track—the group worked to figure out what exactly Cameron Walcot may or may not have done. Cléo dug into the Walcot family's background and found some interesting investments in companies along the way, and positions of power held by family members in those companies as well. Dominique investigated everything that had been written about T.W. Alco, of which there was not much. No one had ever really seen him in person, and he always preferred to do business by phone or through associates. Natalie researched the Young Rising Entrepreneur Competition and found some fascinating results.

Ed and Bo really tried to focus, but ended up catching up with Miss Dina. They learned that she had always been a librarian after school hours for many years, but of course, they had never known until now. Miss Dina was enjoying her new house and still used the grilled cheese recipe the boys had supplied her with so many months ago. But when she asked what was new with Ed and Bo, they remembered they were on a quest.

They returned to the town files and fell deeply into their quest to uncover the source of the Walcot fortune. With each new piece of information, they only had more questions. The Walcot line in the Portland area went back six generations to a Seamus Walcot. They found an aged tale about Seamus returning from a voyage with enough rubies to make his ancestors rich for generations, but they also found some alarming information. They read an old Native American legend that sung the evils and trickery of this man, as he was as slippery as an eel and had been known to have his eye on the Multnomah Tribe's land and treasures. A few reports suggested that Seamus was responsible for forcing the Native American people off of their land. Ed and Bo's hearts filled with sorrow as they read story after story of Seamus' exploitations.

"Dude," Ed said softly. "Why don't we learn about any of this in class?"

Bo shrugged. "I don't know, man."

From behind them, Miss Dina cleared her throat. The boys turned around in surprise to see her peering over their shoulder. "It's because people like Seamus are the people who tell us what we should learn," she said, eyes blazing. Ed and Bo nodded, absorbing the stories before them and resolving to remember the real history from now on. A variety of records and old tombs later, Ed and Bo found another old photograph that swept them both off their feet, even though they were sitting.

"Dude," Ed breathed out.

"It can't be . . . " Bo responded. But sure enough, in this sixty-year old photograph of Hank Walcot, the founder of the Walcot Foundation, there was a very recognizable face next to him. Bo would know that eye-patch and hunchback any-where. They read the caption: HANK WALCOT AT THE RIBBON-CUTTING CEREMONY, PICTURED WITH TOP ADVISOR, TREVOR MILLIGANS.

Ed and Bo looked at each other in surprise. "So this . . . treasure that Spooky Eye-Patch Hunchback is after . . . " Bo said tentatively.

"Could be the same one that Seamus Walcot stole?" Ed answered. Terror Town was on the horizon, and the boys sensed that this was not something that could be dealt with easily. Luckily, Cléo soon stuck her head in.

"It is time," she said gravely. Ed and Bo jumped up to follow her, for the first time glad that they did not have to investigate this particular conspiracy theory. When they all reunited, they were weary, sweaty, and entirely exhausted, but they had a whiteboard filled with information and more than a clue as to what had happened. The group stood in front of the whiteboard that traced the Walcot family's power throughout a multitude of organizations, and they saw just how far the web spread.

"So," Ed said slowly. "The Walcot Family funds the Education Commission, which started the Young Rising Entrepreneur Competition in the first place."

"Right," Natalie answered. "And as such, the chairman of the Education Commission picks the guest judge. And the chairman is, of course—Henrietta Walcot."

"Cameron's mom," Bo breathed out. "And we

have no proof that either Mr. Savage or T.W. Alco are real people."

"But we do have definitive proof that CotLaw is funded through several bank accounts that link to organizations that the Walcot's themselves started," Dominique added.

"And Watloc, Inc. is run by the same executive board as the board that runs CotLaw," Cléo concluded. "And . . . my father . . . " she said softly. "He was a detective. He must have been too close to discovering the truth." They stared at the board in somber silence. There was one name in the middle of the expansive web, one that could connect every person they had met, every adventure they'd had, and every experience they had encountered along the way. In the center of the web was the name, "Walcot."

"So what do we do now?" Bo asked. A long silence fell over the room, a silence that was only broken by the announcement that the library was closing shortly. Ed looked at Bo, and Bo looked at Ed, and they both looked at Dominique and

Cléo. There were only two people here who would not be recognized by the Walcot family. Only two people who would be able to get past the security and make it inside. Only two people who would have a shot at gathering some sort of useful intel.

The boys looked at Dominique and Cléo, and finally, Ed said, "We're going to need you to break inside."

After a few moments of silent confusion, Dominique cleared her throat.

"Uh, break inside what?" she asked.

"Oh, right," Ed said. "The Walcot Mansion. Sorry. Was that not clear?"

"I guess not everyone is in our heads with us," Bo mused.

"Thank god for that," Natalie said gravely.

The group crouched behind the bushes outside of the Walcot Mansion, distinctly making sure not to set off any smoke bombs this time.

"And if, at any point, you feel unsafe, you just hit the alarm button on here and we will come in and get you, okay?" Bo said into his walkie-talkie with gusto.

"Yes, that is fine," Cléo said. "But I do not know why we need to be using the walkie-talkies now!"

"It is hurting my ears," added Dominique. They were all huddled close enough so that the walkie-talkies reverberated some quite painful feedback.

"I also don't know why I don't get a walkie-talkie," Natalie grumbled.

"Because, Natalie," Ed said, "You will be right here with us and can share our walkie-talkies too."

"Well, why can't I go in on the cool mission, then?" she yelled.

"Because they know who you are and you could get hurt!" Bo yelled back. "Uh, sorry," he muttered when everyone turned to look at him.

"Why do we have to wear these outfits again?" Dominique said, gesturing to her all-brown jump-suit.

"I know nothing about deliveries," Cléo added.

"Look, all you need to know is that you have this big box," Ed said, gesturing to the box next to him, "that you have to deliver to Cameron himself. You get in, you see what you can find, you get out, okay?"

Dominique and Cléo looked at each other and nodded.

"Okay, great," Ed said, and then briefly locking eyes with Cléo. He added, "And, uh, be careful in there."

Cléo gave Ed a quick and almost imperceptible peck on the cheek before jumping up and heading towards the front gate without another look back. Dominique followed, turning to wave broadly a few times. Natalie, Ed, and Bo watched them leave, and Ed gripped his walkie-talkie tightly in his hand. Bo slowly put his hand on Ed's back.

"It's okay, dude."

"Yeah," was all he could respond. They watched as Dominique and Cléo buzzed at the gate, and held their collective breath while they waited to see if the gate would open. When it did, they all breathed out a sigh of relief, but this was only the first hurdle. Dominique and Cléo carried their nondescript box up the sloping expanse of the walkway, and before long, they were almost out of sight. Luckily, the group had come equipped with handkerchiefs that were also binoculars, and as such, they were able to see as Dominique and Cléo rang the doorbell. They waited tensely to see who would answer. After what seemed to be an unbearable amount of time, the door finally opened to reveal a well-dressed butler. They exchanged words about something, and then they entered.

When Ed and Bo lost sight of Dominique and Cléo, they turned to each other, eyes wide with fear.

"Maybe we made a mistake," Ed said.

"What if they never come back?" Bo asked. Natalie shushed both of them, using the voice she reserved for hurt animals.

"Guys, it's okay. It's a suburban family's house, not a death trap."

"We don't know that!" Ed yelled back.

"All we can do is wait," Natalie said, and the boys had to agree. They sat in the dirt behind the bushes across from the Walcot Mansion, and they waited tensely for longer than seemed healthy for their poor, young hearts. They waited, and they held their walkie-talkies close to their sides in case the emergency tone sounded. They waited, and they kept their eyes trained on the door. They waited in silence, because everyone was far too nervous to make small talk at a time like this.

"Okay, I'm going in," Ed said when he had waited long enough. "Something is definitely wrong."

"No, dude, you can't!" Bo shouted. "They'll know it was us! It'll ruin the whole thing!"

"Who cares?" Ed yelled back. "We told them to go in there, the best we can do is go in and get them out."

"Remember how that worked out the last time we tried that?"

"Well, we saved them in the end, didn't we?"

"Just barely!"

"Look!" Natalie shouted, pointing at the door. In all of their bickering, they had not noticed when the front door had opened and Dominique and Cléo emerged. Ed and Bo both immediately stopped talking and stared intently at the women, searching for signs of attack. They smiled, chatted, laughed, and looked okay.

"Who are they talking to?" Ed asked, because whatever that person was saying, it was apparently very funny.

"I can't see," Bo said, peering as best he could. But when Dominique and Cléo shifted slightly, both of the boys were able to see just who was being so charming.

"Cameron," Bo spat out, his voice thick with dislike.

"I don't believe it," Ed said. There he was, as

shiny and perfect and well-groomed as ever. He seemed perfectly at ease, as if he hadn't robbed two innocent young men of their entire company and also structured an entire web of lies to make it happen. Natalie spat into the dirt for good measure, and everyone tensely waited for Dominique and Cléo to make their way over to the bushes. After another unbearable length of time, they started to leave. But, before they departed, they both kissed Cameron on each cheek. Ed almost ran out of the bushes in a jealous attack, but Bo and Natalie restrained him. A few moments later, Dominique and Cléo were heading down the path towards them, and the boys were bursting with questions.

"What happened?" screeched Bo.

"What did they say?" Ed asked.

"What was the inside like?" Natalie asked.

"Where did you go for all that time?" said Bo.

"Why did you kiss him?" Ed asked jealously.

Dominique and Cléo, however, did not stop at

their hiding spot in the bushes. They kept walking past as if they had heard nothing.

"Wait!" Bo said.

"Where are you going?" Ed asked. They continued to walk away down the street, and as they did so, they pressed the high-pitched tone that only meant one thing. Ed looked at Bo, Bo looked at Natalie, and Natalie looked at Ed.

"An emergency," Bo said softly.

"An emergency!" Ed echoed. As quickly as they could, they dove through the thick cluster of bushes in order to follow Dominique and Cléo.

7

"**W**hy must we talk out here like peasants?" Cléo yelled over the roar of bulldozers as they stood on top of Montgomery's roof.

"What?" Ed shouted back.

"I said, why must we talk out here like peasants?" she repeated.

"What was that?" Bo asked.

"Because," Natalie yelled, "it's the only place we can be sure they won't hear us!"

"What was that?" Dominique asked.

"It's the only place we can be sure they won't hear us!" Natalie repeated.

"I do not understand!"

Natalie shook her head and shrugged to Ed and Bo. When it seemed as if nobody would be able to hear much of anything, the bulldozers finally died down and everybody could take a refreshing breath of air.

"Plus, we have lawn chairs up here," Bo said as he pointed to the flimsy pieces of plastic that the group was sitting on.

"Yes, very luxurious lawn chairs," Natalie drawled, and Cléo cackled in her seat. Ed eyed the two of them warily, and then leaned in.

"Okay," Ed said, "what happened?"

"Please tell us," Bo said. "I have been dying."

Dominique and Cléo exchanged sidelong glances, and then surveyed the destruction of the old senior courtyard before them.

"What is all of this mess for?" Dominique asked.

"Just a new courtyard, but that's not important," Bo said. "Tell us before they start again!"

The boys eagerly awaited the news, and Dominique nodded slowly, running her fingers through her frizzy hair.

"Well, before we begin," Dominique said cautiously, "I have a strong suspicion that Cameron might be what you call a 'psychopath.'"

Cléo nodded as Dominique spoke, but Ed, Bo, and Natalie gaped back at her.

"Like a serial killer?" Bo finally asked. "That would explain a lot."

"No, not exactly," Dominique said. "I studied psychology in university, and well, I think that Cameron is a highly functioning, well-adapted psychopath."

Natalie nodded as Dominique spoke, unable to stop herself from jumping in.

"Yes! Totally. As you may or may not know, I took AP psych and so I think I can say I know a fair amount about this—"

Ed shook his head vehemently and cut Natalie off. "No way, dude. I've known him since he was a kid!"

"Did he ever do anything . . . strange as a child?" Dominique asked in her thick accent. "Harm an animal or a person or lie his way out of something?"

Ed shrugged defensively. "I mean, everyone does that at some point."

"No, something that is not exactly normal."

As Ed reflected, he could recall once instance in particular in which they had been playing at Cameron's house and they had broken a vase. Cameron had very coolly blamed it on one of the maids right in front of Ed. He didn't speak up, even when the maid was promptly fired. When Ed told the group that story, Dominique nodded knowingly.

"Why is this important?" Ed asked indignantly.

"We are getting to that," Cléo said.

"Hey, guys, maybe we should take a break," Natalie suggested. It was evident how viscerally uncomfortable the two boys were. By a break, she of course meant the joint she held in one hand and the bag of snacks she held in the other, because she always came to a stakeout well prepared. The group exclaimed their agreements, and as they passed the joint around between them, they made an incredible discovery. Whether it was an accident, a stroke of pure genius, or a moment of divine inspiration, Ed and Bo looked over to find Dominique and Cléo dipping their salt and vinegar chips into the jar of peanut butter. The looks on their faces were indescribable.

Natalie almost gagged at the thought of it, but Ed and Bo were intensely intrigued. They slowly reached into the bag and each withdrew a chip, hesitantly arching their hands toward the jar of peanut butter. Tentatively, they each covered their chip with peanut butter, and without breaking eye contact, they slowly put it into their mouth.

It was an explosion of tastes unlike any other they had ever experienced. They were used to their fair share of weird flavors, but the smooth, silent power of the peanut butter perfectly mingled with the aggressive punch of the salt and vinegar to create an entirely novel taste. It was as if the boys could see for the first time, or more accurately, as if they could taste for the first time. They convinced Natalie to try it too, but she wrinkled her nose and spat out the glob of food onto the rooftop, which made everyone laugh. When they all had their fair share of salt, vinegar, and peanut butter, they felt calm enough to get back to business.

"Well," Dominique began, gathering her breath and her courage. "There are certain kinds of people who can do things without having any remorse or second thoughts. These people do not care about others and prioritize themselves over just about everyone and everything else. Some call these people psychopaths, others just call them successful businessmen."

Ed and Bo listened, enraptured. Bo was incredibly intrigued by this theory, and it wasn't just because he hated Cameron, although it was mostly because of that. Ed was still having quite a bit of trouble accepting what Dominique was saying.

"She is saying this because we need to understand

what kind of person we are working with," Cléo said.

"So what happened when you went inside?" Natalie asked. Cléo nodded grimly.

"It seems as if he has everyone under his control."

"Everyone?" Bo asked.

"Everyone," Dominique confirmed.

"His mother and father appeared to be shackled to his every whim, he has an entire array of people to do his bidding, and he controls them all with an iron fist," Cléo said. Bo gasped, realizing the true reason Cameron had been so evil and secretive: he was part iron robot.

Ed noticed Bo's expression, and leaned over to whisper, "Metaphor, man." Bo's face fell, because an iron robot enemy was much more interesting than a plain old spoiled rich dude.

"He is not a good man," Cléo continued.

Ed and Bo thought back to the words Mr. Walcot had mouthed at them, the words that looked strangely similar to, "Please Save Me."

"What did he say to you at the end?" Ed asked weakly. "When he saw you out?"

Cléo and Dominique both paled. Dominique looked down at the floor, and Cléo refused to meet Ed's eye contact.

"He said that he knew who we were," Dominique said, a fury barely contained beneath the surface. "And that he would make it his mission to destroy us if we kept fighting him."

"Just like his people did to my father," Cléo said quietly.

"And he said to tell all of you," Dominique continued, "that he won the day he was born."

At this, Natalie laughed out loud. Everyone grimly turned to look at her, and she continued to chuckle.

"Come on, really? 'He won the day he was born'? What kind of person says that?"

"A psychopath," Dominique responded.

"No, an idiot," Natalie said. "Look. You cannot let this boy intimidate you. Trust me! I dated him for three boring weeks, and while this psychopath stuff is pretty cool, maybe it's a little simpler. Maybe he's just a rich kid who has too much power."

Bo sighed angrily; anything that reminded him that Cameron dated Natalie was viscerally unpleasant. Cléo looked at Natalie strangely.

"You dated this evil man?" she asked.

"But I thought that you are in love with Bo?" Dominique said innocently. Natalie instantly reddened, and on cue, so did Bo. He darted his eyes over to Natalie, wondering if that was true, and also wondering how he felt about it. Ed stiffened in his seat, and everyone had a shared moment of discomfort that Dominique and Cléo missed. Luckily, the bulldozers began their racket once more, and everyone could relax into the sound of grinding metal and lifted-up dirt. As they all sat in the lawn chairs and pondered their feelings and their futures, an important thought struck Bo, as tended to happen every now and then.

"When is the courtyard opening?" Bo asked with fervor.

"What was that?" Dominique asked.

"I said, when is the courtyard opening?" Bo asked once more.

"We cannot hear you!" Natalie shouted back.

"I said, 'When. Is. The. Courtyard. Opening?'" But still, he was inaudible over the cacophony. Finally, he repeated himself at the top of his lungs, just as the bulldozers stopped. His question rang out loud and clear throughout the neighborhood. A bird cawed back in the distance. A car honked.

"I think the ceremony is next week," Natalie said with a shrug. "Why?"

Bo looked at the group of rag-tag spies gathered before him, and at his partner in crime sitting next to him. Ed saw the glint in Bo's eye and knew that this was the beginning of Cameron's end.

"The Walcots are sponsoring the renovation, right?" Bo said.

Ed nodded, the realization dawning on him as well. "That's where we get revenge," he said with a smile.

"In this new courtyard?" Dominique asked.

"No," Bo said. "At the opening ceremony. When everyone in the entire neighborhood has gathered to hear Cameron Walcot speak."

Tiny smiles of subversion spread amongst the group as they sat on the rooftop and envisioned just how extensive their revenge could be, if they executed it well. Ed thought about the betrayal of his childhood friend and knew that he had to strike back. Bo thought about Natalie and wondered if Dominique had been kidding or if that had been something Natalie had said, and how were people even supposed to tell if they were in love or not? Finally, Ed looked at Bo, and Bo looked at Ed.

"We're going to need more back up," Ed said with a smile.

"What?" Bo said over the roar of the machinery.

"Can we go somewhere where there aren't any bulldozers?" Natalie asked.

The boys stood stiffly in Bo's basement, on the verge of addressing their emergency group of future spies. They both gazed out at the sea of former Square One employees nervously. "Hello," Ed said. "And thank you all for coming. It really means a lot to us."

Bo nodded profusely next to him with a large smile plastered across his face.

"As you may know, we have not been delivering for the past few weeks," Ed continued. Before he could keep going, Terry raised her hand from the back. Ed sighed.

"Yes, Terry?"

"I want my paychecks," Terry said. "I worked overtime twice and haven't seen a cent." The group in front of them murmured their agreements. Ed looked to Bo in fear. Terry was a very scary seventh grader to talk to.

"Uh, yes, thank you for your concern," Bo said cordially. "Which is part of why we are here."

Terry raised her hand in the back once more, and Ed accidentally made eye contact. "Uh, yes, Terry. What now?"

"I also want to know why we are here," Terry said. "And why we are in an exact replica of your garage and who those old French ladies are and when exactly you are going to pay us?"

This elicited some cheers from the group of workers, and an offended scoff from Dominique and Cléo at the use of the word "old." Bo held up his hands to quiet them down, and started to write on the whiteboard. Alexandra, the shy one, whispered something in the back. The meeting continued, and everyone ignored her. Terry started talking to Miggy W., the girl with defective tear ducts and the best phone-answerer they ever employed, and the two continued to loudly draw attention away from Ed and Bo at the front of the room. Another hand slowly rose into the air, and Ed wearily called on it.

"Yes, you?"

"Hey," Mitchell said, the sandy-haired boy whom nobody really remembered.

"Uh, hello," Ed said carefully, full aware that he had no idea who this person was.

"How can we help you?" Bo asked blankly.

"I just also wanted to know if we would get those dragon uniforms back. Totally not cool that you guys took those from us."

"That's just the thing!" Bo yelled, gesturing at what he had written on the board: *CAMERON WALCOT*. "We didn't do any of those bad things to you guys. Cameron Walcot did!"

The group quieted for a brief moment, and then continued to yell, perhaps even louder.

"We want Natalie!" Terry began to chant, and then the group picked it up. Alexandra seemed to be saying something else in the corner, but since she was the shy one, nobody heard her.

They chanted, "We want Natalie!" over and over again, and Natalie looked at them, bewildered. She had purposefully told Ed and Bo they needed to handle this on their own, because honestly, everyone had been very close to rebelling before they had gotten shut down in the first place. But now that they were chanting her name, Natalie hesitantly moved to the front to join Ed and Bo.

"I'm here, I'm here," she said, raising her hands to quiet the crowd. However, instead of calming down, the crowd yelled even louder and began to throw items ranging from quarters to tomatoes at her. She yelled and dodged them to the best of her ability until Bo emitted a loud yell. It reached a haunting pitch and raised the hair on the back of everyone's necks. It was a wolf howl. Everybody sat in subdued silence, looking at the man who had created that gut-wrenching sound.

"Listen to me," Bo said earnestly. "We are very sorry you have not been treated right. You did not deserve that. But we asked you here today to promise revenge, and . . . " He paused as he looked around the room, making eye contact with everyone.

"Ask for your help. We can't take Cameron down without you."

"We need each and every one of you in order for this plan to work," Ed added. When Terry started to quickly retort, Ed cut her off before she had the chance. "Look. If you don't do it for us, do it for yourselves. Each and every one of you deserves to have a cut of this company, because we wouldn't be here without all of you. And each and every one of you will get that if you help us."

"What do you say?" Bo asked, afraid of the answer. For a long time, longer than seemed necessary, nobody spoke. Then, ever so slowly, Joseph stood in the back.

"I'm in," he said. "I need to get my hoodies back."

Alexandra was the next one to stand next to Joseph, smiling proudly. "Me too," she declared, and Ed and Bo had to realize that they had never actually heard her speak before. Then came Mitchell, and Ed and Bo wondered again who had hired him and when. Slowly, one by one, the various workers they had employed in the past year stood and looked ahead at Ed and Bo. Finally, only Terry remained seated. She darted her head back and forth at the legions of people standing around her, rolled her eyes, and stood up as well.

Dominique started to slowly clap, but when no one clapped with her, she stopped abruptly.

"I thought that slow-clap thing worked here," she whispered to Cléo, who just shook her head.

"Only in dumb American movies," Cléo responded.

Ed and Bo smiled at the group of warriors before them.

"Thank you," Ed said simply.

"We will not let you down," Bo said. Both boys were on the verge of tears. Looking out at the faces staring back at them, they realized for the first time that this was what the job had truly been about: working with people. After a few moments of quiet reflection, everyone got pretty tired of standing, so they sat down one by one. Bo cleared his throat,

Ed adjusted his shirt, and they turned to the white-board, the object that would always be the preferred platform for plotting and the like.

"So," Bo said matter-of-factly. "The dedication ceremony of the new Interius Montgomery High senior courtyard is in six days. Cameron Walcot will be speaking at the ceremony in front of every-one, plus it will be broadcast on the local news. That gives us six days to figure out exactly how we are going to take down the man who took us all down first."

Ed nodded. "If you look under your chairs, you will find two important items." Everyone bent down and peered under their chairs to find a bag of salt and vinegar chips and a tiny watch. "One of which will guide you through the entirety of this process and keep you safe. The other is a watch that is also a walkie-talkie."

Ed chuckled for a long time at his joke, as did Bo, but the group in front of them was mostly just confused. Dominique raised her hand.

"I don't understand—how will these little chips save us from almost certain death?"

Bo's smile started to falter. "No, that was just a joke. The watch is the thing that will save you. The chips are just a snack."

With shrugs rippling throughout the audience, everyone opened their bags of chips and munched away. Ed and Bo had learned that the first rule of business was to always keep your employees well fed. While everyone enjoyed their chips, even Terry, Bo looked at Ed.

"Are you ready?" he asked with an anxious smile.

"Go ahead," Ed responded. Bo nodded. He had spent several hours coming up with this next part.

"Okay, everybody," Bo said. "We have six days until the event, and we only have one final delivery to make." He stopped and made eye contact with each and every member around the room.

"What's the delivery, Bo?" Ed asked in an uncomfortably rehearsed and stilted voice.

"I'm glad you asked, Ed," Bo responded. "We have a delivery of revenge . . . for Cameron Walcot!"

Silence, save for the continued munch of chips. Not even a single chuckle.

"Oh, come on guys!" Bo said. "That was funny!"

"He spent hours working on that," Ed added. "He thought that would be the line that sold all of you on joining us."

Terry raised her hand once more. "Is it revenge time yet?"

"Soon enough, Terry," Ed answered. "Soon enough."

"Like, right now!" Bo said, standing in front of the whiteboard with the authority of a man on a mission. "We've got a lot of spy ground to cover in the next few days."

"And not a lot of salt and vinegar chips with which to do it, so bear with us," Ed added. Mitchell's hand shot up into the air.

"Yeah, uh, you?" Bo said.

"You could always order more!"

Ed shook his head, and Bo chuckled. "Remember, dude," Ed said, "the whole reason we are doing this is because there is no longer a way to order stuff anymore."

"Really?" Mitchell asked. "My mom definitely got staples from some sort of delivery thing just last week."

"You must be wrong," Natalie said dismissively.

"No, I know she got staples, because before we didn't have staples and now we do."

"Okay, well it couldn't have been Square One," Ed said defensively.

"That was what it was called!" Mitchell yelled. "Square Two."

Ed and Bo gaped at Mitchell blankly. "Excuse me?" Ed finally asked.

"Yeah, it was a demo service for this thing called Square Two," Mitchell said. "Supposed to be revolutionizing the way stuff is delivered."

"Has anyone else here heard of this Square Two?" Bo yelled to the crowd. People made noncommittal sounds of agreement, and Bo turned to Ed angrily.

"That is *so* not cool!" Bo shouted.

"You know what?" Ed said. "We can't *just* take Cameron down. If he's doing this shit, we've also got to re-launch our business. We've got to . . . take on the world," Ed said with gravity.

A few moments of intensely dramatic silence fell over the room, and then Bo sneezed.

"Sorry. Albert again."

"Come on, man! You can't just sneeze like that when I'm delivering such powerful rhetoric!" Ed said.

"Sorry! Tell your cat to stop attending our important meetings, then!"

"I will tell Albert *no* such thing!"

The boys continued to bicker as the wheels of change began to slowly turn, and the revolution started to grow.

For the next six days, the **Square One Team** put their plan for revenge into action. They divided into two divisions: The Secret Spy League and Back to Square One. The Secret Spy League was headed by Dominique and Bo. Members included Alexandra, Mitchell, and Miggy W. Duties involved training on the wide variety of spy equipment, developing a foolproof plan to swindle Cameron out of his pride and money, and also wearing a lot of different disguises. It was a very important job, and luckily it was also very fun. The group ended up smoking spliffs provided by Dominique, and discovering their spirit animals together. When Bo told the others his spirit animal was a wolf, he really knew he was talking about one wolf in particular.

The Back to Square One team was responsible for preparing for the re-launch of the Square One brand. Ed, Natalie, and Cléo led the group, with Terry and Joseph as their reluctant helpers. They returned to the original inventory list Square One had used for their very first launch and developed the basis of their rebranding—the "Back to Basics" Campaign. They stocked Bo's basement with every object they thought a customer could need. No more electronics or touch screens or apps; the service would exist exclusively as a call-in service for their neighborhood area, no more, and no less. They decided to re-nominate the dragon as their official mascot, and added a fire-breathing, red-tailed hawk for good measure. They started advertising as secretly as they could. They painted an outline of a dragon and hawk on sidewalks across the neighborhood with an alphabetic code, that when unscrambled, gave the number to call to order from Square One.

"There is no way this will work," Cléo said as they painted it. Ed shrugged.

"We always liked the smarter customers anyways."

The two divisions worked separately and came back to Bo's basement or Ed's kitchen or the roof of Montgomery High at the end of every day to share their successes, failures, and updates. The Spy League kept close tabs on Cameron, mapping out his every move and location. He did not seem to be tracking their activity, but then again, Cameron had tricked them before. The Back to Square One team trained in biking, speed, and turn-around time to ensure their opening night would go as smoothly as planned.

Finally, the senior courtyard dedication ceremony was the next day, and the two divisions had prepared for the purported demise of Cameron Walcot. Bo wrote the plan on their whiteboard, as all of their plans had always been written.

STEP ONE: Split into The Secret Spy League and The Back to Square One team in order to prepare for the big event. Keep Terry in line.

STEP TWO: Infiltrate Montgomery High on the morning of the dedication. Plant the recording devices accordingly. Keep Terry in line.

STEP THREE: Form the final Division: The Ed and Bo Get Revenge League. Divert and confront Cameron in the designated area. Keep Terry in line.

STEP FOUR: Launch Square One once more as Cameron falls from grace, winning back the hearts and minds of the entire community, and perhaps, the world. Continue keeping Terry in line.

"Sound good?" Bo asked once they had finished writing. The entire Square One Team nodded, even Terry. She was well aware what a handful she was.

"Great," Ed said. "We strike at dawn tomorrow."

"Dawn?" squeaked Bo.

"Well, actually, there's that Earth Day awareness assembly at eleven tomorrow, so that'd be a good time to sneak in," Natalie corrected. Ed shot her a glare.

"I mean *metaphorically* we strike at dawn, Natalie!"

Mitchell raised his hand in the back. "Wait, so are we doing dawn, or eleven?"

"I have track practice at dawn," Terry shouted.

"I have to sleep at dawn," Joseph said. The group descended into bickering once more, but when Bo opened his mouth to howl again, the group quieted instinctively. Natalie shot him a look of gratitude.

"We strike at eleven," Bo said decisively. "But it will be the *dawn* of the Second Coming of Square One; see what I mean?"

Everyone slowly nodded, turning the figurative

language over in their minds. The dawn was near, even if everybody didn't fully understand it yet.

The entire group of Square One operatives stood outside the school, pondering their future but also catching their breath from the walk up the intense incline. The warning bell rang.

"That gives us three minutes to get inside in the hallway confusion," Natalie said. Ed and Bo both nodded, but could not move forward. Not yet. They were about to try to take down the most influential nineteen-year-old they had ever met, and it was a substantial amount of pressure. Ed thought back to Tessa, and wondered what she was doing now, and if she would be proud of him for fighting for what he wanted. He thought that she probably would be, and then he decided to stop thinking of her like she was deceased and give her a call once this whole thing was over. Bo let his mind drift into a little bit of an abyss, and before long, he felt the strength and courage and freedom of a creature on all fours, with limitless potential. He remembered the power and energy of the wolves; that was something he could never forget. As he closed his eyes, he heard Ted's haunting howl echo through his mind. He opened his eyes to see everyone in the group turning around in confusion.

"Where's that howl coming from?" Terry asked.

"Is that a coyote?" Alexandra said.

Bo felt warmth spread through his chest. "You guys hear it too?" They nodded, and Bo knew Ted was truly with them. "We can do this," he said softly.

The group slowly filtered through the front door into the school, and divided into their separate groups as they did so. Finally, only Ed and Bo remained.

"So uh . . . " Bo said.

"Yeah," Ed answered. They both smiled the sad smiles that they had grown far too used to these days.

"Are things going to be okay?" Bo asked.

"I hope so," Ed responded. Bo nodded. He held out his fist, and Ed fist bumped it.

"Good luck," Bo said.

"Good luck to you, too," Ed responded.

"See you on the other side."

With that, they parted ways, walking toward the rest of their future, and hopefully, the end of Cameron's reign.

The Secret Spy League was deep in their preparation, and Bo had never felt more alive.

"How we looking up there, Alexandra?" Bo asked, as she stood on a ladder in the hidden corner of the hallway directly behind the new senior courtyard.

Alexandra said something in response, but Bo could not hear it.

"What was that?" he asked. Alexandra said something once more, and Bo decided that hopefully nothing was wrong. Miggy W. watched from around one of the corners, and Mitchell watched from around the other.

"Remember to make sure the microphone is pointed down below! And the video camera too!" Bo shouted. Just then, Miggy W. called the bird call that could only mean one thing.

"COVER!" Bo whisper-shouted as loud as he could. When Ms. Jeralé walked around the corner a few moments later, all she saw was the headless lower-half of somebody up in the ceiling, tinkering with the lights. She did not even pause as she walked by. When the coast was clear, the group emerged from their locker hiding spots and Bo scanned the horizon.

"Dominique has been gone for an awfully long time," he said to Mitchell, who shrugged. Just when Bo started to think about conducting a rescue mission, he heard the echoing voice of Dominique's mangled Southern accent reverberating from around the corner, as well as the deep authoritative voice of none other than Principal Hunter himself.

"Yes, yes, I quite love to eat pizza and hot dogs while watching football! Those are absolutely my favorite activities besides looking at the flag. Did I forget to say y'all? I meant to say, 'y'all' at some point."

"You just look at the flag?" Principal Hunter asked quizzically. Bo motioned for everyone to resume their hiding spots, holding his breath as the pair rounded the corner. He dove into the nearest locker.

"Oh, did I say look? I meant think about. I'm always thinking about the American flag. And how great it is. And how much I love America, uh, y'all. That kind of stuff," Dominique said. Bo could see through the slats of the locker that she was nervously shifting from foot to foot and struggling to keep her face from forming the French sounds that she was so used to.

"Oh, yes. Very interesting. Well, you really do need to get back to class, Ms. . . . "

"Lockman," Dominique answered instantly as her eyes landed on the lockers in front of her. Bo held back a groan. "Jane Smith Lockman."

"Ms. Jane Smith Lockman," Principal Hunter repeated, with his eyes narrowing. "What class did you say you were in again?"

Dominique started to mumble a mix of words, but just in time, Alexandra clanged loudly on top of the ladder and Principal Hunter ran over to steady it.

"Whoa there, everything okay up there, Bev?"

Bev was Montgomery's maintenance worker who was always perpetually on a ladder somewhere. With Alexandra's head up through the ceiling, she could maybe pull off a Bev if nobody looked too hard. Alexandra grunted a reply back down and Principal Hunter awkwardly took his hands off the ladder, turning and smiling at Dominique with finality.

"Okay, well, good to see you again, Ms. Lockman."

"Likewise," Dominique answered.

"I think that's a long enough bathroom break, don't you think?" he asked.

"Yes, sir, of course."

With that, the two headed opposite directions,

and when the echoes of Principal Hunter's steps receded in the distance, Bo popped out from the locker where he had been anxiously waiting. Dominique returned, eyes wide with stress.

"I am simply not cut out for this sort of work," she said, with pain coloring her voice.

"That. Was. Incredible," Bo said, holding up his hand for a grand high five. "You are spy number one; it's official."

Alexandra, Mitchell, and Miggy W. each grunted sounds of displeasure.

"Sorry, guys, but if you want to be spy number one, you've got to pick up the spying game! We've only got half an hour until the ceremony starts!" When everybody stared back at him without moving, Bo sighed. "Please, I meant, please."

Ed and Cléo kissed with the passion of two people who thought the world might be ending, and for the first time, it was not solely in Ed's dream. They hid in a shadowy corner of the hallways, wrapped up in each other and making up for a hell of a lot of lost time. When they broke apart, Ed gasped for air, because he hadn't exactly figured out yet how to breathe while also kissing. He didn't know if there was something he was missing, and he resolved to look it up later.

"We should get back to work," Cléo said, also a bit breathless.

"Yes. We should," Ed said. But with their faces and bodies so close to each other, there was no resisting another round of passionate making out. The thoughts of confronting Cameron, saving the company, and all of that faded into the back of Ed's mind, and then disappeared entirely. All that mattered was her face so close to his and the smell that he had only been able to remember in his dreams. But then, Natalie walked around the corner and the moment abruptly shifted.

"Ed, we need—Oh, god. Oh, man. Please stop," Natalie sputtered, closing her eyes and stepping backwards. Ed and Cléo broke apart as if an electrical current had shocked the both of them. Neither of them said anything, and everybody reddened quite a bit.

"Okay, look, Joseph has the brownies all ready to go and we just need to switch them, and people are starting to come in for the ceremony, so we should get into our places," Natalie said in one long breath. "That's all. Okay. Goodbye."

When she left, Ed and Cléo looked at each other and burst into guilty laughter at the same time. They giggled as they moved back closer to each other, but before they could get sucked back into the intoxicating world of making out, Ed sighed heavily.

"We really should do this whole revenge thing."

"Yes, we should," Cléo agreed.

He looked at her dark eyelashes and felt the softness of her skin, even though he wasn't touching her at the moment—that's just how soft it was. He glanced down at the red-tailed hawk tattoo on her ankle, and he felt his heart soar.

"Or," he said slowly. "We could just run away together and leave this whole thing behind us forever."

Cléo looked back at him for a long time, her eyes wide and impassive, and then finally curtly shook her head.

"That is idiotic. Let us at least get our money first."

She stepped away from him toward the growing ceremony noise in the shining new senior courtyard, but Ed was paralyzed for just a moment longer. Cléo turned around to look back at him sternly, although the corners of her mouth twitched into a slight smile.

"Are you coming?" Cléo asked. Ed nodded vehemently, and he thought that he could go anywhere that Cléo went. She beckoned for him to follow her, and Ed did, his head held high and his mind drifting back to the imminent attack. Cléo nodded to him on the cusp of the door into the courtyard, squeezing his hand tightly before entering. He stood and stared through the doorway into the gathering reception. Soon enough, Bo came to stand next to him. Parents, teachers, and students filed into the courtyard, and Ed and Bo stood in the middle of them, awash in the activity of the unsuspecting bystanders.

"How's the Secret Spy League?" Ed asked.

"All set up. Alexandra played Bev the Maintenance Worker very well," Bo reported. "And Back to Square One?"

"Supplies are all in place," Ed responded.

"Did you just make out with Cléo the whole time?" Bo asked suspiciously.

"Only part of the time," Ed answered as a blush began to spread. Bo chuckled, and hit Ed on the back.

"I guess it's time, huh?" Bo asked.

"I guess so," Ed answered.

The time for division was over, and all that remained was the final League: The Ed and Bo Get Revenge League. Members included everybody.

Duties included defeating Cameron once and for all. Ed and Bo both felt the nervous energy of a long-shot plan about to launch into motion, and all they could do was roll with it.

9

"The eagle is approaching the nest, I repeat, the eagle is approaching the nest," Dominique's voice rang out through her walkie-talkie watch. Ed and Bo crouched in two lockers next to each other in the hallways surrounding the senior courtyard. They could hear the roar of the crowd begin to grow as the fine people of their neighborhood filed into the school for the dedication ceremony. For Ed and Bo's town, dedication ceremonies were not to be missed. There were baked goods, punch, and sometimes even coffee. Lately the town had been hiring a spunky event photographer named Mandi who published high-quality, glamorous photographs the day after the event. Anybody who wanted to be anybody came to these ceremonies, especially one thrown by the notoriously wealthy Walcots. There were probably going to be at least two large cats of prey, though nobody knew if they would be panthers, or tigers, or both.

Ed and Bo tensed up, holding their breath and preparing to spring out of the lockers in their surprise attack, when Cléo's voice filtered through as well. "Actually, that is not an eagle," she said quickly. "Our mistake. All of these boys look the same."

Ed rolled his eyes and Bo rolled his eyes through the locker wall next to him.

"We never should have had the French girls on lookout," Bo said in a loud whisper.

"Agreed," Ed said.

"Hey!" Dominique said through their watches, because they had left the talk button on.

"Uh, that's not what I said," Bo said quickly. "Or meant. Uh. Never mind."

"And Operation Magic Brownie Switch is a go," Natalie's voice said through their watches. Bo smiled in spite of the overwhelming tension.

"That's a great code name," Bo said.

"Thank you," Natalie responded, in a tone that communicated so much more than just those two words. Bo blushed a little.

"You're welcome."

"All right, all right," Ed said into his watch, readjusting his cramped legs and peering through the locker slats to see the crowd thinning as the start time neared. "He must be getting here any minute. How's it look inside there?"

"Like a new courtyard," Joseph said calmly. "No spiders."

"No spiders?" Ed said. "Can we get a confirmation on that?"

Alexandra said something into her watch about no spiders, but nobody could exactly make it out.

"The courtyard is full and the crowd is growing restless," Natalie reported.

"So am I," Bo said, mostly to Ed. His large limbs could barely squeeze into the tiny-half lockers, and he reminded himself how thankful he was that bullying in high school had taken place online instead of through physical actions like shoving people into lockers.

"Oh! Oh!" Dominique's voice rang out. "We have what appears to be an Eagle Car. I repeat, an Eagle Car."

"What does that mean?" Bo asked.

"We did not agree on any of this code," Ed said.

"She means a limo," Cléo said. "There is a long fancy car and somebody is getting out . . . "

Ed and Bo collectively held their breath, partially out of suspense, but also mostly because there was not very much room to breathe in the locker.

"It looks like . . . a tall blonde man . . . or perhaps a boy . . . "

They tensed even more.

"It is him," Cléo announced solemnly. "The psychopath kind of boy who is so handsome he could probably sell houses."

Ed and Bo nodded grimly. They turned to each other, even though a wall of lockers separated them, and nodded once more. Bo spoke into his watch. "It's go time, everybody. Remember your positions, and remember . . . "

"Hang in there," Ed concluded.

"The eagle is entering the building," Dominique said. "We've lost visual contact."

After a few moments, the echoing footsteps of Cameron Walcot sounded through the hallway.

"The eagle is approaching," Bo whispered into his watch. "Deploy the decoy."

As Cameron's footsteps grew louder and louder, the lighter tread of a youth bubbling with energy and barely disguised rage came from the opposite direction. Ed and Bo peered through the slats as Cameron rounded the corner, clad in a steel-gray suit that really accentuated his steel-gray eyes. Bo thought that Cameron definitely got his teeth whitened, and then wondered if maybe he should do that, too. Cameron carried himself with the ease of a boy who had always gotten everything he wanted, and it was evident in the strides he took that he did not expect anything to ever halt him. Which is why he jolted back in surprise when Terry came running up to him, hair tied in pigtails and generally comporting herself as a carefree youth.

Ed and Bo peered at Terry, waiting for a crack in her disguise; they were by far the most afraid of Terry's ability to perform.

"Mister, mister!" she said in her best impersonation of a poor newspaper seller. "Can I please have your autograph, sir?"

Ed and Bo watched, their hearts beating in their chests. The entire course of the plan hinged on this part going correctly. Cameron peered down at Terry with the effusive smile of someone who expected small children to ask for his autograph.

"Why, hello there!" he said in his crisp and clear voice. "Of course!"

Terry twirled her hair and smiled. "Why, thank you, sir. You are ever so kind! One day, I want to be just like you!"

Cameron smiled and reached toward the paper that Terry held out. "Just stay in school, and you'll get there. And who can I make this out to?"

Terry paused a moment, cracking her Cockney peasant accent for a moment. "Ter– uh, I mean . . .Penny! Penny Pingleton."

Ed and Bo clenched their jaws. Bo felt the contents of his stomach threaten to rise up into his throat, and Ed felt a constant stream of sweat continue to pour out of his body. Ed wiped his glasses reflexively on his shirt. Cameron narrowed his eyes, and peered down at Terry. She shifted nervously.

"Do I know you from somewhere?" Cameron asked.

"No, I think I must just have one of those faces," Terry said. "People tell me I look like Madonna."

Cameron continued to squint, and then nod-ded, a confident smirk growing across his face. Ed and Bo both let out a sigh of relief. They knew what that smirk meant.

"Oh, right, that must be it." He grabbed the paper, signed it in a flourish, and handed it back to Terry in one fluid motion.

"Gee, thanks, mister!" Terry said, and then stepped back a few feet and banged on the locker doors. She continued, "For giving us back our company."

The locker doors swung open to reveal a cramped Ed and Bo, who less than gracefully emerged from their chosen hiding spots. It was not very glamorous and took far longer than anybody had expected.

"Uh," Terry said, stalling for time. "We'll explain it all in just one minute."

Bo had gotten his shoulders out but could not figure out just how to get his legs through the opening. Ed had somehow gotten a shoelace stuck in the locker wall and eventually just decided to take the shoe off in its entirety.

"Any second now," Terry continued. Cameron patiently waited, saying nothing but retaining his confident smirk the entire time. Finally, Ed and Bo removed themselves from the lockers. Ed was down one shoe, but the boys were ready.

"Hello, Cameron," Bo said aggressively. "So good to see you again."

"Likewise," Cameron answered, with a polite tip of his head. "And Ed," he said, turning his head to make eye contact with Ed. Ed stared back, his blood boiling, and then settling into cool adrenaline.

"Cameron," he responded curtly.

"And what's all this about you 'winning back' your company?" Cameron asked pleasantly.

"Glad you asked," Bo said, his smile growing. "If you remember back to two minutes ago, you signed an autograph for poor little Penny Pingleton, over there," he said, gesturing to Terry in the corner.

"But," Ed said, "what you didn't know is that Penny is actually Terry, our best delivery person at Square One."

"Another thing you didn't know," Bo continued triumphantly, "is that you didn't just sign any piece of paper. You signed a contract, my friend."

"One that gives up your control over Square One and gives it all back to us," Ed said.

"So, in conclusion," Bo said, "always read the contract."

"It's just the smart way to do business, dude," Ed added for good measure. Ed, Bo, and Terry beamed triumphantly back at Cameron. But, after a few moments had passed, Cameron began to clap slowly and incredibly sarcastically.

"Oh, well done," he said. "Well done, indeed."

Ed and Bo's smiles began to falter as Cameron clapped louder and louder. Terry shifted nervously.

"Yes, thank you, it was well done," Bo finally said after this went on for quite a few minutes.

"Oh, my dear Ed and Bo, if only you two could

see beyond your own stupidity, you would be able to appreciate this moment right now with me."

"I'm appreciating this moment all right, thank you very much," Bo said, crossing his arms and moving a few steps closer to Cameron. Cameron finally ceased his sarcastic laughing.

"Who do you think taught you the whole contract thing in the first place?"

"Paolo Müllers," Bo answered quickly. Ed continued to stand back, simmering in his cool rage and waiting his turn for a decisive jab at victory.

"Wrong again, boys. It was me! It was me the *entire* time," Cameron said, his smile growing. In the shadows of the hallway, the boys could hear the rumble of the crowd in the courtyard just beyond the window, but they could not be seen. Terry shifted nervously, and pointed to the contract again.

"But we've got you! We've got your signature and we've got the company back!"

Cameron smiled and shook his head in the most condescending way possible. "Terry, Terry, Terry.

Do you really think I would forget a troublemaker like you? So talented, but such a bad attitude. We could have used somebody like you, you know."

Terry shrank back a little, handing the contract to Ed and turning away. She headed around the corner and into the courtyard, leaving Cameron laughing as she left.

"Ed, could you do me a favor and read my signature on that piece of paper your little Penny was so kind as to get me to sign?"

Ed looked down at the contract in his hand, his blood boiling once more. He struggled to keep his voice calm, because they were so close. An outburst now would ruin it forever.

"You've been duped," Ed read softly. Cameron beamed and chuckled once more.

"Thank you, thank you," he said, straightening his tie. "Now do you see why this is all so funny? You've lost, my boys."

"We haven't lost anything," Bo yelled. Ed might be able to restrain himself, but Bo had no such qualms. He ran up to Cameron, sticking his chest out as far as it could go and staring into his cold eyes.

"We're going to get our company back," Bo yelled once more. "Whether you like it or not!"

Cameron wiped a few drops of spit off of his face, and took a step back. "Please, not before my speech." He started to walk past Ed and Bo as well, but Bo moved into his way, blocking him.

"You had no right to do any of that to us," Bo said. "No right. This is all ours, and one day, everyone will know that."

Cameron tried to side-step Bo a few more times, continuing to smirk.

"Please, give it a rest. I've got a speech to give and adoring fans to shake hands with."

Bo looked back at Ed, nodding his head in indication that it was time. Ed slowly stepped forward, the hair on the back of his neck standing up as he pulled a vial out of his pocket, slowly opened the top, and continued walking toward Cameron. Bo was busy distracting Cameron by being a moving body blocker, and so, Cameron was none the wiser when Ed reached over and tipped the vial down Cameron's back.

"What the—" he said, and then jumped and yelled as loud as he could. "What the hell?! What is this?"

"The spiders you displaced from the courtyard wanted to thank you personally," Ed said calmly. Sure enough, a vial's worth of spiders were traversing their way around and over Cameron's back, sending him into a fit of jumping, swiping, and yelling. Ed and Bo both cackled in amusement. If there was one thing that could unnerve Cameron Walcot, it was spiders. After more than a few minutes of spider removal, Cameron turned to Ed and Bo, eyes blazing. They both smiled back calmly. They had trained six whole days for this moment.

"You guys are both pieces of shit, do you know that?" Cameron spat out. "Do you know how easy it was for me to destroy you?! From the very beginning, it's been me calling the shots, and you have had no clue the whole time," he said in one big breath. "I've been Mr. Savage. I told the French Mafia to kidnap those stupid French girls. I planted those market shifts and those contracts and got the company rightfully from you two *freaking* idiots."

He paused for a moment, catching his breath and straightening his tie. "I've been controlling the trading *this whole time*. Do you know how many companies the Walcot Foundation owns? No, of course you don't," he cackled, and his eyes landed resolutely on Ed. "My dearest Ed, so trusting, yet, oh so idiotic. Well, guess what? I've been manipulating you for *your entire life*. Ever since that first day at Sunday School, you've just been a stupid little pawn in my scheme. *Nothing* in your life has been yours," he said, panting heavily.

Ed asked the question that had been troubling him this entire time.

"Why?" he asked simply. Cameron laughed caustically.

"You really don't remember?"

Ed shook his head, glancing at Bo.

Cameron narrowed his eyes. "Kindergarten. The park. The day you and Bo met, because Bo hit you in the head with that ball? Ring any bells?"

"So what?" Ed said.

"So?" Cameron spat out, laughing maniacally once more. "Ed, *we* had been playing together at the park right before that. *We* knew each other from Sunday School. You didn't even invite me to play with you guys. If it weren't for that stupid ball, Bo wouldn't even be here right now."

Bo slowly cleared his throat. "So, are you saying that you did all this shit because you were . . . jealous?"

Cameron spat on the ground in anger. "Of course not. I did it because I could, and because I deserved this success, and because you two are *idiots*."

With that, Cameron walked past them and out into the thunderous applause of the crowd waiting for him. Ed and Bo both slowly breathed in and out, turning to watch through the window as Cameron waved and smiled and prepared to give his speech.

"Dude," Ed said slowly.

"I know," Bo said dreamily. They turned to each other, and smiles broke out across their weary faces. They high fived.

"I can't believe that worked!" Ed said.

"I know!" Bo repeated.

Through their walkie-talkie watches, the voice of Natalie spoke. "Alright, and Operation Secret Confessional Projection, you all set to launch?"

"Set," Mitchell said.

"Set," Miggy W. echoed.

Ed and Bo looked at each other and smiled. At the same time, they took a breath, and said the words that would end it all. "It's go time."

"Please!" Natalie said quickly, as Ed and Bo both breathed in deep breaths in order to yell at each other. "Do not jinx on this. It's all I ask of you. Now is not the time."

Ed and Bo shrugged, and yelled jinx anyways, because some things they could not give up. As they wrestled at the soda machine in the hallway, the voice of Cameron rang through the courtyard and the whole school behind them.

"Hello, thank you all for coming! It's a pleasure to be here, and it's a pleasure to be representing the people of Interius Montgomery High."

Ed was the first to procure a soda from the machine and present it proudly to Bo, demanding that he owed him a soda. Bo groaned and forked over the two dollars for the drink, lamenting that he really had to start playing dirty.

"As you all know," Cameron's voice continued. "I've had the extreme pleasure of becoming CEO of one of the fastest rising local businesses, and as of this morning, I have been named CEO of Walcot Enterprises." This was met with thunderous applause, and in the pause that followed, the voice of Cameron rang out once more, but not in the speech-giving kind of way. Ed and Bo ran to the window with the soda, ready to toast to the end of a Cameron-dominated era.

"You guys are both pieces of shit, do you know that?" Cameron's voice rang out through the loudspeaker. Cameron stopped onstage, smiling nervously and searching for the source, but the sound just continued. *"Do you know how easy it was for me to destroy you?!"* Cameron's face fell into a ghostly white, and he tried to yell into the microphone.

"That's all for today, thank you for coming," he said, but the entire crowd was riveted by the sounds of Cameron announcing his evil plans to the world. Ed and Bo smiled through the window as all the teachers, friends, and neighborhood residents began to scowl and boo Cameron. They watched as Belfroy stood up and yelled, and soon enough, the entire crowd followed. Cameron ran offstage as the sounds of his confession echoed through the school, and ran past Ed and Bo.

"You've been duped, my friend," Ed said calmly. Cameron looked at them, eyes blazing, and then turned and stormed out without another word. Ed and Bo only had a few minutes to revel in their success, because then it was time for the launch of Back to Square One. Natalie had jumped onto the stage as the recording ended.

"Thank you very much, everyone, for coming," she said. "Please, please, *please* do not hesitate to take one or two or five brownies on your way out."

Ed and Bo entered the pristine, airy courtyard and gingerly took the podium with Natalie.

"I'm Ed," Ed said simply.

"And I'm Bo," Bo said. "And we're Square One."

"The real ones."

"Tonight, we will be launching our Back to Basics campaign."

"No smart phones," Ed said with a smile. "No emails, nothing like that. Give us a call and we'll get you what you want."

The crowd applauded loudly and Ed and Bo beamed out at their former peers, teachers, and neighbors. The boys were back.

10

It had been Joseph's idea to switch the regular brownies at the dedication ceremony with pot brownies, and their plan hinged on his stroke of culinary-minded genius. The neighborhood residents returned home, confused and a little bit sad about what Cameron Walcot the Wonder Boy had revealed himself to be. It was the deepest hope of everyone at Square One that an hour to an hour and half later, depending on how full their stomachs had been, the residents of their neighborhood would get the munchies. Until then, they waited.

Ed, Bo, and the entire Square One team returned to Bo's house to await the Second

Coming. Four/Freddie had heard the entire broadcast, and proudly announced that he was quitting the security guard business to pursue his passion of becoming a veterinary technician. He was officially Four no longer, and he unlocked the garage once and for all.

"And . . . the police have taken Cameron into custody," Natalie said, eyes glued to the TV coverage. "He's charged with . . . eighteen counts of fraud, insider trading, tax evasion . . . " Natalie continued to name every charge, but Ed and Bo stopped listening at a certain point. All that mattered was that the people finally knew the truth. Cléo stretched in anticipation of the deliveries to come, and turned to Ed with a softness in her eyes.

"And are you okay?"

"What do you mean?" He asked.

"That thing about Cameron controlling your . . . whole life?" she asked tentatively. Ed shrugged.

"Worse things could've happened. At least my life included all of you guys," he said in an uncharacteristically heartfelt moment. Everybody murmured an, "Aww," even Bo.

"Cut it out!" Ed laughed.

"We love you too, buddy," Bo said.

"How does it feel to take down the biggest enemy that you never knew you had?" Dominique asked with a wide grin.

Ed and Bo both considered this for a moment, then turned to each other and shrugged.

"It feels okay," Ed said.

"That's it?" Cléo asked in astonishment. "This man ruins your lives and your families and your garage and that's all you can say?"

Ed just shrugged once more, and Bo nodded.

"I feel kind of empty," Bo said. They had been working for so long toward this one singular goal, and now that it was accomplished, they really just felt okay.

"He was really lonely, in the end," Ed said softly. "At least we have each other."

"And salt and vinegar chips," Natalie said, passing

the bag to Bo and smiling as their hands touched. Now that all the spy business was mostly over, the boys could return to their more pressing desires and instincts, like smoking, eating, pooping, and being hopelessly in love with the women in their lives. Bo smiled back at Natalie, feeling the same fluttering in his chest that never seemed to go away, no matter how hard he tried to not think about her when he watched porn.

Meanwhile, Ed was sitting in a beanbag chair next to Cléo and continuously replaying that fateful night in that hotel room so long ago. He had been so young, so naïve. Now he was a real man; he had run a business in New York, gone to college, dropped out, and everything. He felt more like a real person, but still very much like a real person who did not know how to express his real feelings. So, he sat in silence next to Cléo, viscerally aware of how the sides of their legs were touching but unable to say or do anything about it. For her part, Cléo had her eyes glued to her phone. Ed wondered if she was actually just as shy as he was, but when she turned to look him intently in the eyes, he twitched and looked away quickly. No, she wasn't shy; she just was not nearly as self-conscious as him.

The rest of the Square One gang talked, argued, or chatted as the case may be, and everyone felt giddy in the aftermath. And since a watched kettle never boils, everyone was nearly startled out of their seats when they heard the first shrill ring of the phone. It rang once, it rang twice, and then Ed slowly rose to his feet, walking to the table in the center of the room with the corded phone on it. The eyes of Bo and all the rest of the Square One Team on him, he answered the phone.

"Hello, thank you for calling Square One, Ed speaking. What do you want?"

As the munchies spread, the orders grew, and the Square One team responded. It felt a lot like the good old days, except Ed had learned to treat his employees better, Bo had learned to focus more, and there was a lot more sexual tension between everyone. They let all thoughts of the past and the future fade away, and for the stretch of evening hours in which people were home and wanted things but did not want to go out to get them, Ed and Bo delivered. It wasn't about profit or rules or stock or any of that, it was purely and simply about getting people what they wanted.

In the days that followed, Ed and Bo had a lot of hurdles to jump. The Cameron Walcot scandal became local, and then regional, and eventually even national and international news. Ed and Bo were a huge part of both the media frenzy and the legal proceedings that followed. The secret confessional inspired federal probes into Cameron's tax history, which revealed a whole host of crimes and discrepancies. Cameron was tried for an array of crimes that Ed and Bo did not really understand, but they went to court and shared what they knew, leaving out some of the details about the weed usage. The French Mafia toppled soon after, and all the major players and newspaper spy men were apprehended in the French court system thanks to the information Ed and Bo provided.

The Square One team started to see changes almost immediately, as the freeze on their accounts were lifted and they were able to pay their employees for the weeks of work that had never been accounted for. A police investigation into the Walcot Mansion turned up Joseph's favorite nondescript, slightly stained gray hoodie, and he tearfully reunited with his true identity. Ed and Bo were able to get the DeLancey house back in order, just in time for Ms. DeLancey to return from her business trip.

Ed and Bo were sitting on the tried and true thrift store couch, relaxing and enjoying the space that they had missed so much, when the garage door slowly opened. A sleek sports car pulled into the driveway, and Ms. DeLancey stepped out, clad in a form-fitting suit that made her look surprisingly a lot less like a mom. She carried a distinct platinum briefcase with her.

"Hi, honey!" she called in the voice that reminded Bo that she was indeed a mom. "How have you two been?"

"Oh, just fine," Ed said. "Nothing crazy happening here."

"Wow, yeah! Nothing crazy happening with me, either," Ms. DeLancey said with a well-rehearsed smile plastered over her face. Natalie stepped out into the garage with a ginger-ale in hand.

"Sup, Mom. Nice wheels. Did you find Dad?"

"What?" Ms. DeLancey asked, her voice dropping into an octave they had never heard before. "Who told you about that?"

Natalie and Ed exchanged glances of an accidental discovery. "Uh, I was just kidding," Natalie said. "Just a joke."

"Oh," Ms. DeLancey said, her voice returning to its normal pitch. "Of course! Yes, nothing crazy happening here, like I said." Ed and Bo noticed the bright red ruby earrings and the ruby-studded band she was wearing on her finger. It may even have been on her wedding finger, but the boys could never remember what finger that was supposed to be. Bo's eyes darted to the platinum briefcase, and noticed the striking similarity between the cases he had found in his house. Ms. DeLancey quickly walked into the house, firmly gripping her briefcase and avoiding eye contact.

"Dude," Bo finally said, his brain ordering every clue in line for the first time. "I think your parents might be spies."

Natalie laughed, but Ed just shrugged.

"I think yours might be too," Ed said.

"Seriously, guys?" Natalie asked skeptically. "Not everyone we know is a criminal mastermind. Least of all *Mom*."

"Think about it," Bo said. "The whole thing with your Dad leaving; the treasure map we found; the Eye-Patch Hunchback; the Walcot Fortune; your mom's business trips and meetings with suited men . . . Dude, open your eyes."

"Well, you straight up have a spy closet in your house," Ed countered. The boys looked at each other for a long moment of contemplative silence, and Natalie rolled her eyes.

"Do you remember how we became friends?" Bo asked.

"You hit me in the head with that ball at the park."

"The one that our *parents* dropped us off at," Bo finished. "Spies *love* the park. It's the least conspicuous place there is."

Ed and Bo stared at each other, allowing this information to sink in. Natalie scoffed from near the door, but the boys ignored her.

"So, that means that my dad didn't actually leave us, he just went away on spy business?" Ed asked hesitantly.

Bo looked into Ed's eyes and nodded. "And whenever my parents leave," Bo said, "they're going on missions, not just long vacations without me?"

"And just maybe," Ed said softly, "they've been trying to reclaim the treasure that the Walcot family stole this whole time?"

Natalie stared at the two boys and shook her head, but Ed and Bo were too caught up in their thoughts of spy-parents to notice. She went back inside, and after a few more moments of quiet contemplation, Ed and Bo went back to the important matter at hand—discussing the costs and benefits of those shoes that had wheels on the bottoms of them. So far, neither of them were exactly sold on the whole idea.

A few days later came the farewells to Cléo and Dominique. The boys were distinctly not ready to say goodbye. But, as Cléo said, it looked like the boys could handle themselves from here on out. Ed and Cléo had shared a few private nights together before Ms. DeLancey returned home, and he found himself feeling a hell of a lot of things he had no idea how to combat. The best he could do was smile and think about the words "I love you," and wonder if he would ever have the courage to say them again. Ed and Bo drove Dominique and Cléo to the airport, and Dominique and Bo chattered the whole way. They set up plans for the next visit and demanded that they all stay in touch. They covered the silence so that Ed and Cléo could sit next to each other and bask in their shared company for just a little bit longer. When they finally reached the airport, Bo and Dominique took the bags inside to the check-in, giving Ed and Cléo some much needed space.

"Well," Ed said, his voice catching in his throat, "I guess this is it."

Cléo nodded, and stood on the tip of her toes to lean in and kiss him. Ed kissed her back, reaching his arms around her and doing his best to remember every curve of her body, the stylish cut of her hair, and the way her stark eyes softened sometimes in the right light. When they broke apart, she smiled.

"This is not the end, Ed. This is not it at all."

She turned around and walked into the airport, and Ed stared after her. In the car ride home, Ed and Bo didn't talk at all, but Bo took them to the Taco Shack drive-through to treat Ed to some much-needed tacos.

"You okay?" Bo asked as they munched on their crispy-shells and headed home.

"Yeah," Ed said simply. "I will be."

Bo nodded. He knew what that felt like.

Before anybody was prepared, it was time for Natalie's graduation. It was a graduation like any other—a lot of strangers and their families mutually agreeing to sit through a very long ceremony. Ed, Ms. DeLancey, and Bo all cheered as loud as they could when Natalie's name was called. She looked into the stands and smiled, waving and holding her diploma high above her head. Ms. DeLancey held a graduation party at their house afterwards, and the entire Interius Montgomery High crowd was there to celebrate in style.

Ed and Bo, for their part, distinctly avoided everyone and stayed at the back of the yard next to the fondue pot. They looked out at the sea of youth before them and ate as much fondue as they could possibly stomach. It was quite a bit.

"Dude!" Ed said, when an important thought struck him.

"Yeah?" Bo asked.

"It's been a year," Ed said importantly.

"Uh, a year since what?"

"Since we officially opened!"

"Oh. Cool," Bo said as he shoved a giant marshmallow covered in chocolate into his mouth.

"Do you know what this means?" Ed asked.

"No?"

"Come with me." Ed led Bo into the garage, where they were most comfortable, and sat down at the Square One filing cabinet. He began leafing through the vast array of bills and receipts and reports, typing numbers into a calculator as he went.

"What are you doing?" Bo asked, but it fell on deaf ears. Ed murmured to himself, counted, typed, and finally looked at his calculator, smiling in disbelief. He slowly held up the calculator to Bo, who read the amount out loud. "One," Bo said, "what does that mean?"

Ed laughed. "That's the amount we've made in the past year."

"One million dollars?!" Bo screeched. Ed shook his head.

"One thousand?" Bo asked, his excitement rapidly dropping. Ed shook his head once more.

"Uh. One dollar?"

Ed nodded and burst into laughter, and soon enough, Bo joined him. When they were finally calm once more, Ed cleared his throat, tears of laughter streaming down his face.

"Well, I guess we have to keep running the business," he said, not altogether sarcastically.

"Oh. Shit. Yeah," Bo answered. Both boys thought back to their long-ago pact that they would continue with Square One if and only if they made a profit in their first year of operation, and now, technically, they had. Ed looked at Bo, and Bo looked at Ed.

"I have no idea what the hell I want to do," Bo finally sputtered. Ed shrugged.

"Me neither, dude."

Bo grinned, and moved quickly to a wrapped

box in the corner of the room. He picked it up and turned to Ed.

"Okay, I know your birthday isn't for a few days, but I got you something," Bo said, holding out the package. Ed opened it with gusto to find the DinoBong, whole once more. Sure, it was chipped, kind of dirty, and seemed to be very structurally unsound, but it was back together again. Ed stared at the DinoBong, and then looked up at Bo. All he could do was stand up and hug Bo in one long, tight hug. When they broke apart, both boys cleared their throats and shuffled a bit until the sound of Ms. DeLancey yelling "Cake!" drew Bo towards the door.

"Shall we?" he asked.

"One more thing," Ed said, as the words tumbled out of his mouth rapidly. "I'm sorry I was such a dick about you dating Natalie. I, uh, I mean . . . It's kind of awesome." He peered down at his feet intently for a few moments. "I guess what I'm trying to say is that it's okay with me," he murmured.

When he looked up, he saw the bright face of Bo beaming back at him.

"Okay," Bo said. "Thanks."

When Ms. DeLancey yelled "Cake!" a second time, the boys headed out into the yard to hover in the back of the party once more.

Later that night, Ed, Bo, and Natalie found themselves on the rooftop of Interius Montgomery High. They had ostensibly returned to retrieve their lawn chairs, but a few beers lifted from the graduation party had made their way into Natalie's possession. Now they each sat and contentedly sipped their drinks, gazing out at their neighborhood domain.

"You are totally going to ruin college," Ed said to Natalie.

"How can somebody 'ruin' college?" Natalie asked indignantly.

"I don't know, but you'd probably find a way to do it."

"Ed, maybe you should transfer to Georgetown

and be Natalie's roommate," Bo said in a sarcastic drawl, which elicited loud bursts of laughter from the entire crew.

"Yes, please live with me, Ed," Natalie said in a monotone. "I just simply do not get enough of your effortless graces at home."

Ed shoved Natalie and Natalie shoved him back, and before long, they were all laughing. When the physical rigor of the rooftop exhausted them, they lay down on their backs, gazing up at the cloudy night sky.

Bo reached over and grabbed Natalie's hand, his heart thudding in his chest and threatening to burst. She smiled the sort of smile that spread into her eyes, and squeezed his hand back.

"What do we do now?" Bo asked.

"I don't know," Ed responded.

They lay on the roof of their old high school and watched the clouds pass by in the night. The whole sky stretched above them, and the whole world lay in front of them.

EPILOGUE

"**N**o, dude, you just really don't get it," Bo said angrily as he took a small puff, emitting a few well-rounded circles of smoke. "I *know* that ferrets cause happiness, because I gave Teddy a ferret for Christmas and she was *so* happy."

Ed chuckled as he reached over and grabbed the joint from Bo. "But how did you buy Teddy that ferret?"

Bo fell quiet a moment as Ed took a long, celebratory hit. "Money, I guess," Bo murmured eventually. Ed laughed as he exhaled his smoke, but Bo just shook his head obstinately.

"That doesn't prove your point! You don't win!"

"Whatever, dude," Ed responded. "All I know is that my lab is just like, weeks away from perfecting the Velocidactyl."

Bo turned to Ed, his eyes glistening. "Really?" he asked.

Ed shrugged, adjusting his tie and brushing the salt and vinegar crumbs off his shirt. "I'm really not at liberty to discuss."

"Oh, come on, man!" Bo said, running his hands over his clean-shaven head. "You can't leave me hanging like that!"

"Alright, I'll tell you on two conditions," Ed said.

"I'm listening."

"Number one, you come visit me in Tokyo more often."

Bo smiled. "Done. What's number two?"

"You promise me that you will not give my niece *another* small rodent for her birthday."

Bo's smile faltered slightly, and he held his head high. "I simply cannot promise that."

They continued to bicker about the merits of small-rodent ownership, Velocidactyls, and the like when Natalie stuck her head through the door. Her hair was long and flowing, framing a very weary, but very content set of eyes.

"Dinner time, guys," she said.

"God, Natalie, for the last time can you please just *knock* before you enter!" Ed said, a smile playing across his lips.

"Nope," Natalie said. "We are too old for that. I am a mother. You are not a child anymore."

"That was funny!" Ed insisted. "Back me up, Bo."

Bo shook his head firmly. "I plead the Fifth."

"You cannot do that every time we argue," Ed complained.

"I can when it's an argument between my best friend and my wife!"

"You don't see me bringing *my* wife into all these arguments!" Ed retorted.

"That's because you don't have a wife anymore," Bo said with a smile.

Natalie stepped back inside, shaking her head as she went. Some things never changed.

"For the last time, technically I do still have a wife," Ed responded. "Every time we meet with the divorce lawyers, she just says, 'This still isn't over,' in that impossible-to-resist accent, and then we make out."

"She's a weird dude, man," Bo responded.

"You can say that again," Ed said wistfully.

"She's a weird dude, man," Bo repeated with a smile. Ed leaned over and pushed Bo, and Bo pushed back. But before a full-on fake fight could ensue, the men began to feel the rising hunger of very forceful munchies. They put out their joint, stashed away their supplies, and cleaned up the garage, returning Ms. DeLancey's woodworking materials to their rightful place. In the years that her children had been gone, she had decided to overcome her fear of the activity, and had recently been creating benches and chairs that were all studded with rubies. She had also given up her globe fandom in favor of a real job. She was curating the Multnomah Tribe Museum that had opened a few years prior, funded entirely from an anonymous donation of recovered Multnomah jewels. She did, however, take up a new hobby of crafting tiny boat replicas. Whenever Ed had asked her about what the boat thing was about, she had wistfully smiled and answered, "They remind me of your father."

The boys stood on the threshold of the door, about to enter into a dinner of canned food and a sea of small ships, and paused for just a moment.

"Dinner!" Ms. DeLancey's voice rang through the closed door. Ed looked at Bo, and Bo looked at Ed. The two hesitated for just a few more moments, because in the garage, they could always be kids.

"Same time next year?" Bo asked with a tentative smile.

"Same time next year."